DEAD MEN'S FINGERS

DEAD MEN'S FINGERS

by

Tyler Brentmore

Dales Large Print Books
Long Preston, North Yorkshire,
BD23 4ND, England.

British Library Cataloguing in Publication Data.

Brentmore, Tyler
    Dead men's fingers.

    A catalogue record of this book is
    available from the British Library

    ISBN   1-84262-194-7 pbk

First published in Great Britain in 2002 by Robert Hale Limited

Published in Large Print 2002 by arrangement with
Robert Hale Limited

Dales Large Print is an imprint of Library Magna Books Ltd.

Printed and bound in Great Britain by
T.J. (International) Ltd., Cornwall, PL28 8RW

Thinking of Bruce and Rex and Jeremy
out there playing
Paddy O'Shea

ONE

The street torch flared as Wharton turned into the alley, his shadow stretching in front of him before melding with the darkness caught between the buildings. He paused to belch, reaching out a hand to steady himself against the rotting clapboard. Part of his winnings had gone on an extra bottle, and part on feeling up that new whore of Molly's. Little cat had tried to take him to one of the back rooms, but he wasn't so drunk that he was a fool. He'd leave her 'til he was sober. A man needed to get his money's worth, and that new one looked worth his money.

Sure of his gait now, he headed for the patch of black that crowded the door to the flop-house. He'd nearly made it to the step when someone called his name. A shape as dark as the Devil eased out from the wall to stand silhouetted in the torchlight.

'Bin a long time, Wharton. Keepin' well, I hope.'

There was a sharp scraping and a lucifer flared. Wharton saw the face beneath the broad brim and dragged in such a breath that he nearly choked on it.

'You!'

'Yeah, me, come back to haunt yer just like I promised.'

The hand lowered, pooling the match's flickering light along the waiting gun-barrel. Wharton stumbled back, his bowels as unsteady as his legs.

'No! Weren't me. Were Baddell. Were Baddell's notion, all o'it.'

'That's what the others said. Didn't save them neither.'

The lucifer faded and the gun roared.

TWO

Vern was grizzling again, wanting to hold on to his pa's leg. Jed Longman eyed first the stream of saliva cleaning a course down his youngest son's dirty chin, and then his eldest standing in front of the canvas tent.

'Does he wanna go?'

'No, Pa. He's bin. Reckon it's his teeth agin.'

'Well, just take him, will yer, and let a man converse here.'

Jed removed his hat and pushed his fingers through his unkempt hair. If it weren't one thing it were another. All around him among the tents, families were greasing wheels and repacking wagons the way they'd done each and every day since signing on and being allotted a place. Nerves, Jed had told Tom, folks doing nothing, just filling time. His

11

eldest had nodded sagely, showing more understanding than his nine years gave him credit for. Jed was aware of him now, holding the hands of his younger brothers, waiting on his reply. And here he was, doing nothing, just filling time.

The wagon master shifted his weight. 'Mr Longman, I'm not asking you to agree nor–'

'Agree!' Jed slapped his hat across his thigh and, casting a glance over his three boys, ushered the man away a step. He kept his voice low but gave it the venom the request deserved.

'This here might not seem much to you, Fremont, but it's a godfearing family, and no godfearing family o' mine is gonna give wagon-space to some painted whore who thinks she can pay her way out West–'

'Goddamn it, Longman, you're not listening with both ears. You mention that sort of talk in Mrs Harris's hearing and I'd wager you'd be on your way to the druggist.' Colonel Fremont pinked a little behind his whitening whiskers and let some of his bluster dissipate.

'Mrs Harris speaks real well, more like you'd associate with a school-ma'am. Got all the attributes, *all* of 'em. Comes up to me all prim-like, looks me straight in the eye and asks to join the train.' He leaned into Jed to give more weight to what he was saying. *'On her own.* Needless, I gave her short shrift – a woman on her own, indeed – and I thought that would be the end of it, but no, she's back faster than the flux. Wants me to introduce the two of you – *formally introduce* is what she said – and she won't take no for an answer, Longman. She's there when I water my animals, there when I sit down to my meal. She was there this morning when I came out the shitter still buttoning my pants!'

'Then she ain't no lady,' Jed stated.

'Sometimes, gentlemen, ladies have to go to inordinate lengths to get a hearing.'

The two men wheeled round. From the way Fremont had described her, Jed had expected a fleshy, middle-aged frump with a ramrod back scowling through a pair of pince-nez spectacles, but the woman who had sneaked up behind them was willowy and younger than himself. He'd been right about the back, though. She held herself tall in her high-collared store-bought dress, and despite its ribbon fastening, the hat was prim enough for any woman used to standing before a chalk-board. Fremont hadn't exaggerated a jot about her fierce gaze, neither.

'Mrs Harris...' spluttered the wagonmaster.

'Good day to you, Colonel. I'm obliged to you for interceding on my behalf. Eventually. As we've got this far, would you be good enough to introduce us, please?'

'Er...' Fremont seemed to deflate. 'Mr Longman, Mrs Harris.' As she turned Jed's way, the wagonmaster took a step backwards in escape. 'I'll leave you two good folks to get acquainted.'

There was no bob of her head in acknowledgement. Instead Mrs Harris stepped forward to offer a lace-gloved hand. Jed supposed it only right to accept it under the circumstances, but became acutely aware of the dirt ingraining his knuckles. It had been a while since the soap had seen the scrubbing brush. Martha would have sure given him an earful.

He pulled himself up short and fixed his hat back on his head. 'No.'

'I beg your pardon, Mr Longman?'

'The answer's no.'

'You haven't heard the venture.'

'There's no room–'

'–at the inn?'

He eyed her a moment and it was she who averted her gaze.

'Mr Longman, I'm not asking for living-space in your tent nor to lade your wagon with my belongings. I have my own horse and two pack-mules, and I am perfectly capable of making the journey as an independent rider.'

'Then why don't yer?'

'For the same reason you are travelling

with other wagons, Mr Longman; safety in numbers and the services of a guide. If I were a man there wouldn't be a problem. Alas I am not, and Colonel Fremont carries a very low opinion of the moral fibre of the family men who have signed to his command. He will not have me sign unless I can affiliate myself to a family for *protection.*'

Jed raised an eyebrow.

'Mrs Harris won't be a bother, Pa,' Tom offered.

Without turning, Jed waved his son quiet.

'Why us? There be plenty of others here, an' they got women fer company.'

'There's a natural hierarchy in a family, and a woman does not like to share her kitchen, nor her cooking-fire.'

Nor her man, Jed mused. Mrs Harris was a thin 'un, true, and although he was trying hard to keep his eyes on her face, she had all the right curves in all the right places and a smell about her that he hadn't had in his nostrils for many a day. No, his instinct had been correct from the start. Mrs Harris,

16

school-ma'am or not, was a barrel o' trouble he could do without.

'On the other hand,' she continued, 'an upstanding man like yourself with three young boys could do with some female help–'

'What you trying to do, lady? Tell me that I'm some preacher's son or tell me that I can't take care of my own kin? We've done fine all the way here and we'll do just fine all the way yonder, so go take yer fine talk and pester some other fella.'

Tom stepped forward. 'But Pa, Ma always told us that it was a person's Christian duty–'

Jed swung round on his eldest. 'You take your ma's words in vain and you'll feel my belt.'

Tom stood his ground. 'I ain't. I'm remembering what she said.'

With no one holding his hand Vern's grizzling rose a pitch and then he began to sob. Jed glanced at him and realized that his youngest stood alone. His six-year-old brother was no longer standing in front of their tent. Jake had eased round to Mrs Harris and was holding her hand and whispering, all wheedling smiles.

'Well, Jacob, I might have a piece in my purse if I look hard enough,' the woman was saying to him, and out from the lace wrist-bag came a bundle of twisted barley-sugar.

Jed felt his jaw sag, then gritted his teeth. 'What is this?' He turned back to his eldest for explanation, but Tom's defiance had fled and he was being eyed through lowered lashes.

'You give this piece to Thomas, now, and we'll see if Vernon can be comforted.'

'Enough, lady! Are you trying to bush-whack me through my own children? I'll not have it!'

Mrs Harris was already round his arm, hunkering down beside the crying youngest, who threw his chubby arms around her neck.

'It's not like that, Mr Longman. I met them on the boardwalk outside the Mer-

18

cantile. The storekeeper was chasing them with a broom for leaving sticky fingerprints on his windowpane. Vernon fell and grazed his knee.' Disentangling herself from Vernon's arms she drew a kerchief from her purse and wiped his eyes, cooing to him low and steadily. It didn't seem to have any effect.

Tom sidled up beside his father, his cheek bulging with candy and his eyes glittering. 'Mrs Harris told the storekeeper to pick on someone his own size. Threatened to take the broom offa him and whack him over the head wi' it.'

Mrs Harris looked mortified. 'I did no such thing, young Thomas! At least …not in so many words.' She adjusted her bearing and turned back to Vernon, removing her glove to smooth her hand over his face.

'I don't care what happened,' Jed thundered, 'it ain't gonna buy you a travelling-place with this family. Tom, get your brothers in tow. It's time we fed the oxen and milked the cow or we'll be eating in the dark.'

'Mr Longman, we need to speak.'

'We're done speaking, lady. Just leave.'

He was surprised to feel her hand on his arm, and attempted to shake it off, but her grip became stronger. 'Lady–'

'Vernon!' she hissed. 'How long has he been like this?'

Jed looked into her widened eyes and then beyond her shoulder to where Tom was trying to pull his youngest brother to his feet. There was a sudden empty feeling in Jed's gut.

'It's his teeth. New teeth coming through. Takes him like this.'

'This is not his teeth, Mr Longman. He's running a fever and his throat is raw. Has he vomited? When did he last eat?'

He glanced at Tom, remembering the boy telling him that Vern had pushed aside his morning vittles.

'You know what this means, don't you, Mr Longman? If the Colonel realizes you've a sick child he'll not have your wagon take its place at daybreak. You'll have to wait for

20

another train to assemble, if one does this late in the season. You could lose a month. Like as not you'd hit the mountains in the first snows and lose all three–'

'I know what can happen, lady.'

'Well know this, Mr Longman. Even if you get past Colonel Fremont's assembly to-night you aren't going to be able to keep a sick child a secret. Your wagon will be quarantined behind the rest, and the cattle, and the milk-cows, so your boys will be choking on everyone's dust.'

'All right, all right!' He was well ahead of her and didn't want to hear it coming from her mouth. One sick child could as easily turn into three and there would be no way he could do all the chores, act the nurse-maid and goad the oxen. Not on his own.

Mrs Harris released his arm and straight-ened her spine, stepping back into her school-ma'am regime. 'This meeting was meant, Mr Longman. You have need of a temporary minder for your children and I need to reach my husband. I suggest we accommodate each other.'

This sudden intervention of a shadowy Mr Harris caught Jed by surprise. He'd taken it for granted that she was a widow-woman.

'Do we have an understanding, Mr Longman?'

Jed cast around for alternatives, but there didn't seem to be any. 'I guess.'

He let her take Vern into the tent away from prying eyes and quietly brought the medicine-box from the wagon. Jake was more than happy to stay close to Mrs Harris to do her bidding and, picking up pails and fodder, Jed and Tom made their way beyond the encampment to where the animals were being kept.

'What's matter with Vern, Pa?'

Jed squinted down at his son and decided that a lie just wouldn't do. 'Don't rightly know yet, but if anyone asks it's his teeth, hear me?'

The boy nodded, though his face had become pinched beneath its grime. Jed squinted at him some more. Being the eldest Tom was the only one who remembered all the deaths: Jo-Ann and Charlotte. Then baby Liza. Finally Martha. No, not Martha. They'd been gone two days, he and Tom, checking on the trap-line, and for some reason, for some heaven sent reason he'd left Tom to water the horses and had entered the house alone. He shuddered as the pictures burgeoned in his mind. Death wasn't going to enter his life again and take his boys. He wasn't going to let it.

With his free hand Jed clapped Tom on the back. 'Vern will be fine. We got Mrs Harris takin' care of us now.'

In their absence Mrs Harris had been taking care of more than Jed anticipated. Father and son returned with buttermilk to find their blankets airing on a line and sweepings from the tent in a pile beside the emptied midden pail. The tin tub Martha had used to bathe her babies was by the embers of a fire and every mug and plate they owned seemed to be upturned beside it, dripping water. Jed and Tom exchanged glances and Jed set his shoulders. They hadn't been gone an hour and the woman was taking over. He slapped his hat on the tent-pole, flung back the flap and bowed to enter.

'Mrs Harris–'

'*Mr* Longman, your boys have *lice,* which probably means you and Tom do, too.'

Jake was sitting with his back to the tent wall, his damp hair plastered to his head from a central parting, the chin of his shining face resting disconsolately on his pulled-up knees. Jed bit on what he intended saying and looked across to where she was squeezing out a folded cloth to drape across Vern's forehead. He, too, was cleaner than Jed had seen him for many a day, but whereas Jake's face glowed a little pink, Vern's was as white as the porcelain dishes Martha had coveted.

'How is he?'

Mrs Harris softened. 'Easier. I think the washing tired him out. I've given him a draught of fever-cure. Once I'd got a cup to his lips he wanted more and more. The boy was drying out. I put water on to boil – the scum on the well-water here is a nightmare; it's a wonder the entire encampment isn't sick – so if he wakes in the night he's only to be given from this jug. It should be cold by then.' She turned to him fully, her un-buttoned sleeves rolled to her elbows, the sky-blue dress dirtied across the shoulder and skirt where Vernon's grime had left its mark. 'And how long, sir, have the boys been sleeping in their day clothes?'

'Pa…'

The warning call from Tom was as wel-come as the dawn and Jed took the oppor-tunity to escape Mrs Harris's frosty glare. Tom, he knew, had lent an ear to the one-sided conversation and, despite the differ-ence in their ages, they exchanged a knowing look. Jed rolled his eyes by way of explanation and taking a few good strides away from the canvas muttered, 'Changes faster than the wind, that woman.'

Tom smiled in return and gestured down

the rank, but Jed had already seen the wagonmaster. In the growing gloom Colonel Fremont was with Moynihan, his second, doing their final tally. Whistling through his teeth, Jed glanced towards the tent.

'C'mon, boy. Chores to do and food to cook before we can turn in. Let's make it look an everyday event.'

By the time Fremont was striding towards their fire, stars were twinkling overhead and bacon and onions were sizzling in the pan.

'My, that smells good,' the wagonmaster intoned as he drew level. 'Makes a heart glad, it does. Cured by your own hand, I'd say. Am I wrong?'

'Naw, yer ain't wrong.' Jed cast a guarded look at the wagonmaster and his smiling second. 'We still on fer tomorrow?'

Fremont's affability waned somewhat and he leaned over the firelight to read the paper in his hand. 'Yes, yes. I'd hoped for others joining but every year the numbers grow less. You drew number seven, so you're nearly half-way down the line. A week an' yours will be riding point. No more dust in your craw.' He paused to welcome a remark but when none came he cleared his throat and continued. 'The call is four a.m as scheduled. You got a timepiece?'

Jed pulled his dented watch from his vest pocket and marked the hour from the Colonel's fancy silver fob.

'Pleased you ran off that harridan, Longman. Can't abide an uppity woman. Wanting to join the train on her own account. Have you ever heard such a nonsense? First hard rain and she'd be squealing like a–'

The tent flap opened and out walked Jake in a linen nightshirt several sizes too big for him, Mrs Harris bringing up the rear.

'Now Jacob, say goodnight to your father and quick to bed.' Jed suppressed a smile and reached out to poke at the bacon. 'Ah, Colonel Fremont, I'm pleased to have seen you. Mr Longman and I have reached an accommodation so I won't be needing to sign for the passage on my own account.'

She smiled at him as winsome as any woman could and pushed Jake towards his father. 'Little Vernon is at last sleeping soundly. Such excitement for tomorrow. I never thought he'd fall. He wants me to allow him to ride Snowball, but I told him you'd have to give permission, Mr Longman.' She fluttered her hand. 'But that can wait until the morrow. Come now, Jacob, your father's waiting.'

Jed left the pan and offered a hand to his son. He was surprised how forcefully the little man flung his arms about his neck, fit enough to choke him, and he wondered how long it had been since he'd held his boys.

Mrs Harris came to his rescue, pulling Jake away and ushering him into the darkness of the tent. The wagonmaster cleared his throat and Mrs Harris turned to him. 'Yes, Colonel?'

He tapped the paper in his hand. 'By the terms agreed I have to account–'

'Ah, you want me to sign after all. Why didn't you say?'

'Er, no. It, er, it'll wait until the morning. Good evening to you both.' He touched his hat and turned sharply right, Moynihan following faithfully at his heel.

Jed rose from the fire. 'Staring him down like that was a sight for my eyes. I swear you could hold a hand of poker.'

Mrs Harris rolled down her sleeves. 'Tawdry card-games hold no fascination, Mr Longman. I'll get my hat and be seeing you on the morrow. Mark what I said with little Vernon.'

There was bacon for her in the pan but he didn't mention it. Instead he watched her walk away between the ranks of wagons, losing sight of her in the dim pools of fire-light. Leaving Tom to eat her share, he lit the stub of a candle and checked his younger boys. Jake slept peacefully, his face that of an angel. Vernon whimpered in his half-sleep, his eyelids flickering. Jed took the brow-cloth and damped it in the bowl before laying it back on his son's burning forehead. Mrs Harris had given him a draught. There was nothing he could do but wait.

He looked about the small tent, its mildewed corners, its patched seam. Something brilliant in its whiteness caught his attention, and he lifted the edge of a flour-sack to pull clear one of Mrs Harris's lace gloves. He held it a moment, feeling its softness in his fingers, then he brought it to his nose and breathed deep. It was true that he needed her help at the moment, but he also knew that having her so close was going to be a strain.

He sat there minding his sick boy and staring at the flour-sack long after Tom had rolled himself in his blanket and begun snoring, then all of a moment it was as if the tiredness drained from him.

Mrs Harris had cleaned the tent. Mrs Harris had taken the blankets outside and probably everything else, too. She'd rummaged through their belongings to find Jake a nightshirt, but even so her glove was where it shouldn't have been.

He eased himself closer to the sack and quietly emptied its contents. At the very bottom he brought out a bundle wrapped in oilskin. He held it a while, feeling its weight, before uncovering it in the candlelight. The Peacemaker drew effortlessly from its holster. Had Mrs Harris held it? Had she touched the seven dead men's fingers notched in the rosewood handle?

THREE

Jed had spent half the night listening in the darkness to his youngest son's ragged breathing, and half the night bathing the boy's face in the light from the flickering candle-stub. Somewhere between he figured he must have dozed, because he awoke with a start to the sound of movement and whispered talking beyond the canvas. Striking a lucifer, he consulted his timepiece. Thirty minutes yet to the call, but this was the day of the jump and everyone was eager. He cast an eye over his three sleeping sons and tried not to think too hard of possibilities.

The animals had been fed and watered and the cow milked by the time Mrs Harris stood silhouetted in the rays of the breaking sun. Jed didn't recognize her at first glimpse. Even Tom stood and stared. The store-bought dress had been replaced by a dark woollen jacket and a skirt rising half-way up her calves. Tall boots with riding-heels poked from beneath, and in her hand she carried a wide-brimmed hat not unlike his own. Mrs Harris moved closer, and guiltily Jed snapped his gaze up to her face.

'I said, how has he been?'

'Restless. Slept the night, though.'

'Slept the night or you slept and didn't hear him?'

Jed narrowed his eyes but swallowed the retort fighting its way across his tongue. It was Tom who spoke up. 'Pa kept the vigil. I saw 'im.'

Mrs Harris looked from one to the other and then nodded. 'So by noon you'll both be sleepwalking and then who'll tend the oxen?'

A small scrubbed face emerged from the tent. 'Me!'

Mrs Harris smiled. 'Well young Jacob, ox-tending is a man's work so you'd better come out here and eat the man's meal I spy your brother is preparing for you.' She swept a hand through his hair as he shuffled past trailing the over-long nightshirt, and both Tom and Jed watched the peculiar swing of her skirt as her backside disappeared through the canvas flap.

'What's she wearin'?' whispered Tom.

'Reckon it's a riding-astride rig.' He'd seen sassy young girls riding astride wearing striped bloomers and boots, but not a grown woman in such a length of skirt. He glanced at Tom then flicked his ear. 'You're too young to be lookin'! Git your brother and me some vittles afore we hit the trail half starved.'

Jacob rubbed at his eyes. 'Pa, can I put my pants back on now?'

After her accusation that he couldn't be trusted to tend his own sick child, Jed was of a mind not to offer her a plate, but Mrs Harris busied herself carrying the sleeping-blankets into the wagon to make up a bed for Vernon on top of the crates and barrels, and she never even looked their way. By the time she had made him comfortable beneath the wagon canvas and was striking the tent, even the pan had been licked clean. There was nothing else to do but earth up the fire and put the oxen in their yokes.

Despite the early hour a group of towns-folk had journeyed out to watch the wagons set off and, sitting tall on his grey stallion, Colonel Fremont played to his audience by riding up and down the line. Sometimes he urged his charges to greater progress, sometimes he rode quietly by, one eye on each family's preparations, the other on the fancy watch held high so none would miss it in his hand.

'Don't know what the rush is all o'a sudden,' muttered Tom. 'Bin sitting here nearly a week.'

Mrs Harris leaned against the reins of her animals as she walked them down the side of the six oxen. Her saddled chestnut walked easily, but the laden mules needed tugging. 'Is that a new hat he's wearing?'

'Sure is. But don't give him no comment

on it. He's got 'is speech all rehearsed about how a clean white hat is the best signalling device known to man.'

With a wry smile Mrs Harris continued pulling her beasts to the rear of the Long-mans' wagon. Jed was there tying on the cow.

'Good piece of horseflesh. Sure you'll be able to handle it?'

'Horses I'm used to, it's mules I'm wary of. Oxen I have no experience of at all.'

'Then me and Tom, we'll have to be teaching yer.'

Jed took the lead rein of one of the mules and dragged it round to the other side of the wagon. 'We'll have to separate this bunch or the mules will try to kick lumps out of the cow.' He was going to say more but his gaze alighted on the far side of the chestnut's saddle. Sprouting from the leatherwork like feathers from an Indian's head were two silver-inlaid rifle-butts.

'My husband's,' Mrs Harris explained, but she didn't offer to show him.

A rider cantered down the line, Fremont's second calling the day. Mrs Harris climbed aboard the wagon to cradle Vernon while Jacob sat on the seat with instructions to hold tight. Goad in hand, Tom stood by the head of the ox-team. Jed uncoiled the long, rawhide whip. Fremont stood in his saddle, wasting time jawing to the townsfolk. At last he whirled his white hat, then he drew his pistol and fired into the air. Pulling back his arm, Jed sent the rawhide snaking towards the clouds. The crack, sharper than from Fremont's gun, resounded overhead, followed every second or so by others from along the line. Oxen bellowed, mules brayed, horses whinnied. Children screamed with excitement or fear or merely to startle the draught-animals into forward movement. Wagons creaked, wheels turned. The train was heading West.

They stopped at noon. Vernon awoke and Mrs Harris managed to force down him a little broth she had bottled, but he remained listless and sweating, his snuffles and whimpers a concern. When the wagons moved again he slept. With a finger of light left in the sky Fremont finally drew a halt for the day. The wagons swept into a circle tight enough for each to be linked to the next by chain to create a corral, and all animals were loosened for tending. Fires were built beyond the circle, tents erected alongside. Before long the smell of cooking drifted on the breeze and the wagonmaster and his second began their rounds, allotting guard duties to the men and sampling the families' meals. Jed didn't invite them to sit at his fire, and he found he had drawn the midnight watch.

'And you, Mrs Harris ... how did you find our first day? The creeks were no more than a puddle, eh? The trail almost as smooth as the sky.'

Jacob was leaning against her side, his eyelids drooping as she stroked his hair. She smiled at Fremont, but offered no conversation.

'And your boys, Mr Longman?' He looked

round. 'Three, ain't yer got?'

'Yeah, three. One already asleep, one a-falling, and one' – Jed looked towards his eldest – 'kinda sore feet, yeah?'

Tom took his cue and grinned as if embracing a family joke. 'Yeah,' he said, and Fremont and his lap-dog moved on.

'Won't allus be so easy,' muttered Jed, watching them depart, 'especially as we move up the line. I hear Fremont's wagon rides point and stays there. Some excuse about it containing road-building implements so can't take its turn at the back.'

'That's probably why the man seems to have no food of his own,' Mrs Harris mused.

'He's got plenty all right. I reckon he's saving it for the mountains. Be interesting to see if he's as willing to share with others then.'

'Well, that's a good stretch away yet.' Mrs Harris began to move. 'Take this one, and let us check on Vernon.'

Jed carried the drowsing boy to his blanket

and leaned over his youngest.

'Eaten?'

'Not enough to call it food.'

'Is there any sign–'

'No swellings, no rash, just the fever and reddened throat, but that doesn't seem to be developing.' Mrs Harris rinsed the brow-cloth and bathed the boy's face. 'Mr Longman, you can't nurse him, and stand guard, and handle the ox-team tomorrow.'

'I'll manage.'

'And the day after, and the day after that? You'll be asleep on your feet and likely fall beneath the wheels, and where will the boys be then? Be reasonable, Mr Longman. Take my tent and sleep while you can. I'll stay with the boys.'

'When will you sleep? You look all in.'

'I can sleep tomorrow in the wagon, can't I?'

Horses and mules were driven into the corral and the cattle left to pasture beyond the circle. Jed took Mrs Harris's tent and wished he hadn't. It smelled of her. He eyed the saddle-bags piled along the tent wall but dismissed the notion. She'd gone through their belongings, sure, but this was hardly the same. Instead his gaze rested on the dual rifle cases and he reached out to pass his hand over them. Strange to have two, even stranger their feel beneath his palm. He drew one, its weight surprising him. The silver-inlaid stock belonged not to a rifle but to a peculiarly shaped scattergun, its barrels one atop the other. Even in the gloom he could make out their etching; fancy, like Fremont's watch. The other gun was lighter and oddly balanced. It was not until it slid sharply from its case that he realized the barrels had been shortened, shortened considerably.

Jed caught some shut-eye but it didn't seem long before he was called. Sallis, one of his fellow guards, was as skittish as a colt. Holding his weapon at the ready as if a bayonet was attached, he twisted this way and that at the slightest sound from the herd, convinced that Kaw or Pawnee were lurking in the darkness ready to scalp every man, woman and child. The other guard, Petersen, tried to calm him by saying that he doubted there was a hostile within four days' ride. Jed took a different route.

'You pull the trigger on that long piece o'yours and it'd better be a Pawnee or a Kanzor that catches the lead, 'cos if it ain't you'll be dancing from a rope come sun-up, an' I'll personally see to it that you're left face up on an ant-hill for the buzzards.'

The watch passed without incident.

And so it continued day after day, the Longmans' wagon moving from seventh to sixth to fifth to fourth, each time seeing more of Fremont on his stallion waving his shiny white hat and exhorting greater speed. Jed and Mrs Harris fell into an almost monotonous routine, passing with the barest of words at meal-times, he and Tom tending the animals and Jed doing his stint as guard, she cooking the food at noon and sundown and caring for Vernon through the long night, to cradle him in the wagon during the day. By the sight of her, though, she wasn't getting a lot of rest, and Jed became mindful of the constant jarring of the wagon over the sun-baked ruts, the sudden drops into holes in the broken road. Only the most elderly, he noticed, sat on the wagon seat behind the ox-team. Even the two heavily pregnant women he'd seen preferred to walk for their comfort. He doubted Mrs Harris was getting any rest at all, yet she never complained or shirked a duty taken on. The fierce school-ma'am role had been shucked like harvested corn, but Jed had learned no more about her than he had at that first meeting. Throughout, Vern seemed no worse nor no better, and Jed didn't know whether to be thankful or fearful for the outcome. Jake was checked each morn and night, but seemed as spritely as ever, collecting pebbles to throw at the oxen and keep them moving.

It was part-way through the noon stop-over on the fifth day that a commotion lit through the line of wagons. There was a distant rifle-shot and someone shouted that they'd heard whooping. Everyone went into a flurry of panic. Mrs Harris grabbed her scatterguns and a saddle-bag and bundled a protesting Jacob under the wagon – he wanted to see the savages ride by – but it quickly became obvious that they were being approached not by Kaws or Pawnee, but by three white men desperately sig-nalling with a red under-shirt and clinging to a broken-down mule. Riders were sent out across the undulating land and the men brought in. Folks clustered round as they were given first drinking-water, then coffee, and then bread and plates of food which they devoured as if ravenous hogs. Their mud-encrusted clothes and whiskered jowls full of dirt were commented on by one and all as assumptions were raised and coun-tered. Jed kept his peace, unable to make anything of the dishevelled men. They'd only one firearm between them and not a hat to ward off the sun.

'Mighty kind o'you folks, mighty kind. An

44

answer to a man's prayers, y'are. True as my witness stands, seeing yer is a gift from the Lord.'

His name was McIntyre, he said, 'an' we're all that's left, we are, of six men and twelve mules.'

'Indians?'

'Injun? Haw, no. Worse than any feathered mongrel. The Devil himself, it was, mesmerizing us with lights in the heavens. Beautiful, it looked, too. The most awe-inspiring thing I ever did see.' He squinted at the faces crowded about him. 'Yer didn't see it? The storm?'

The emigrés glanced from one to the other, murmuring surprise. Jed looked from the blue sky with its line of faint grey clouds crowding the western horizon to the dry and compacted ground beneath his boots.

'South, south-west o'here. Maybe five, six nights?' prompted McIntyre.

Fremont squinted down at him. 'Been fair weather all the way, mister.'

McIntyre shook his head as if he couldn't

believe it. 'Well, I guess… Sure thought we were a safe distance, and to be certain we never felt a drop o'rain. Watched it well into the night, we did, until it beat itself to death, and then we took ourselves to our bedrolls.' He shook his head again, his gaze staring into a memory.

'So what happened?' someone prompted.

'What happened? Don't rightly know. Sam was shouting and the mules were kicking and the ground was shaking and … and the next moment we was in the middle o'the ocean being pounded by waves and rocks and bushes an' such.'

There were gasps from the travellers and Fremont slapped his hat across his thigh. 'Flash flood,' he pronounced. 'Ain't I been telling you folks that we got to make time while the weather holds fair? Big rivers lie ahead and their feeders can turn really nasty.'

McIntyre continued, waving his arms as if reliving the event. 'The mule passed me and I clung to its tail. Saved my life, it did. By sun-up there was hardly a muddy puddle to suck into a dry throat, but everything was gone. Everything. Came upon Sam first. Drownded he was, though not a bit of water near him. Sheer luck I met up with these two. The others … the others we ain't seen hide nor hair of, nor the mules, dead nor alive. We figured we were within striking distance of the trail an' hoped to cross with it and come upon some travellers, but it took longer than we reckoned. We sure gives praise on seeing yer canvas.'

'It's a sorry tale, to be certain,' Fremont intoned, 'and we'll say a prayer for those lost, but I have to tell you gents that we ain't got enough in this small caravan of ours to take you right through.'

There were cries of dismay from all around, especially from the women, but Fremont refused to be swayed.

'Good folks,' called McIntyre, 'we appreciate your concern, we surely do, but travelling West is the last place we want to be heading. Some vittles, a couple of canteens and we are making for the sunrise. We talked it over. Working as a drayman seemed to have no future afore this, but now it seems just what the Lord maintained for me...'

Jed felt a tug at his arm and found his middle boy at his side, surreptitiously gesturing back along the line. The hairs rose on Jed's neck and, giving Tom the word to stay and listen, he eased himself from the crowd and walked as quickly as he could allow himself to their wagon. As he climbed up behind the seat Mrs Harris pulled back the canvas. She was smiling as if she'd never smiled in her life before, and such a weight lifted from Jed's shoulders that he thought he would float.

'He's awake and asking for food – and for you.'

Jed squirmed in beside her and touched his boy's face. Vern's hair was sticking to his head still, and there was no colour in his cheeks, but he smiled at his pa and held out a hand. Jed hugged him close, then hugged him some more, hiding the tears of relief springing to his eyes.

McIntyre kept glancing behind until the wagons became no more than a raise of dust. Once again the sod-busters had done them proud, feeding them up to their eyeballs and filling a sack with victuals like it was someone's wedding – no thanks to Golder. McIntyre slapped his palm sharply across the back of Golder's head.

'What were you thinkin' of back there, keepin' yer head down, an' leavin' the jawin' to me? An' don't you ever refuse to take the sack again. I bring you along because o'that hang-dog look–'

Golder swung round, delivering his fingers into McIntyre's throat with the speed of a striking hawk. The older man went down, whooping for breath and turning blue in the face. Scholl let go of the mule, set to intervene, but a glimpse of Golder's knife made him back away.

'Do that to me again, McIntyre, and it'll be this blade you'll be feeling, not my goddamn hand! What you know can be fitted in a woman's purse along with yer half-ass prancing. One of them wagons is carrying a regulator for the Johnstone Freightin' Company.'

'So what's that to us?' demanded Scholl.

'To us, nuthin'. To Baddell, a hellova lot.'

His share of the food ignored, Baddell leaned across the rickety table to peer at his scouts through his one good eye.

'Longman, eh? Thought I'd shaken that buzzard.'

'So you know this nester?'

Baddell snorted, pushing himself back in the only chair the crumbling sodhouse possessed. 'Longman ain't no nester. Last time I laid eyes on his carcass it were wearing a town coat with a fancy vest an' carrying papers saying he was the law.'

'Maybe he still is,' offered Scholl. 'We been pushing our luck on this trail, I reckon. These wagons ain't worth the sweat. All of 'em's pulled by ox and they ain't got over fifty head o'scrawny cattle and a couple o'dozen horses an' mules. It ain't worth the sweat, I tell yer.'

Baddell rocked forward in his chair and swept his arm across the table, sending a jar of peaches to the floor. The glass shattered like an exploding shell. 'You ain't worth dog-puke but I carry you, don't I?'

He strode out of the hole that had once served as the doorway, the men moseying after him at a safe distance. Others were sharing the food from the sack. In the corral milled horses and mules, occasionally baring teeth or kicking out at one another. On the slopes beyond, cattle grazed on the spring grass as if it was their purpose in life. Baddell leaned on the fence-rail and McIntyre leaned beside him.

'Worth taking, boss, 'specially if the weather helps, but Scholl's got a point, too. These critters are rested and gettin' feisty. We got buyers waitin', an' a man doesn't look for a pair when he's holding near a full house.'

51

Baddell faced him, pointing to the eye-patch and fingering the lightning-shaped scars streaking from below it. 'An eye for an eye. Ain't that what the Good Book says? I'm owed here, and you're forgettin' what the pair's worth. Wife an' kids, Golder says, an' wife an' kids always count as aces high.'

It took another two days for Vernon to feel strong enough to sit for a while with Mrs Harris on the wagon seat. When Colonel Fremont saw him there he gave a cheery wave and nothing was said.

Their wagon moved position with each morning's bugle, and each morning brought an ominously darker band of cloud in the sky. Fremont exhorted the wagons to move faster, halving the mid-day rest. The first spots of rain quietened the grumbles. A river was ahead, and if they didn't cross it before it rose they could lose a week or more camped beside it. At last the cry went up. The river was within sight. Tom and Jake ran ahead for news.

'There's a ford,' Jake hollered, 'an' they're gonna double-team the wagons up the bank.'

'Darn it,' Tom muttered. 'Of all the days to be riding last. We'll be waiting for ever.'

'Won't be that long,' their father countered. 'Besides, first across will have tired animals. Ours will be rested.'

Four wagons were taken across without mishap. The back axle of the fifth sank into the churned bank and had to be levered out. Rocks were dropped into the mire to help give it stability, but the work needed to be renewed every third wagon so the older children were set to collecting ballast. Jed was helping goad the double teams into the water when Jake ran up hollering.

'Pa! Come quick, Pa! Tom's afighting! Yer gotta come, yer gotta come *now!*'

Jake was so insistent that his father waded ashore. Not far into a patch of stony scrub was a group of children. Some were looking stunned, a couple were crying, but most were whooping and jeering. Jed could see fists flying above bobbing heads, but his grimace turned to anger as he drew close enough to see the full scene. Stones were being hurled by onlookers and Tom was desperately trying to fend off a boy a head bigger than himself, while a younger cohort was creeping up behind Tom with a rock held as a weapon.

Jed ran across the open space and caught the younger assailant by the wrist, jerking the rock from his grasp and his feet from under him, twisting him in the air so he was catapulted into his elder brother. They both went down like skittles, and with a screeching and screaming the onlookers dropped their stones and fled.

'What the devil's goin' on here!' Jed roared.

Tom flinched away but Jed caught his shoulder and turned him round. His right eye was a bloody pulp. His lip was burst and there was blood running down his chin seeping into his shirt. Jed thought at first that he was cowering, too, but realized that he was covering up, protecting injured ribs. He went down on one knee not knowing where to touch. 'Gee, Tom...'

'Pa ... I didn't–'

'Goddamn it, Longman. What have you done here?'

Jed turned an eye on a barrel-chested man pounding through the low brush, a gaggle of kids and parents in his wake. Brookner, the man's name was, and now Jed had seen him he recognized his boys. Their wagon was a good way up the line from his own.

'Stopping a bushwhacking is what I've done. Don't you teach yer kin to fight fair?'

'I teach my kin to protect one another, and I guess that's what happened. Kids calling each other names and you wade in–'

'Weren't calling me names, Pa,' Tom rasped. 'Callin' Mrs Harris.'

Everything was quiet for a moment and then the Brookner boys scrambled to their feet to stand grinning behind their father. Jed cold-eyed Brookner.

'What's this about Mrs Harris?'

Brookner set his face and pointed a finger. 'Now, don't you go getting yerself all puffed up. You think no one's noticed? You creeping outta her tent to join the watch? Her creeping outta yours on a morning afore the call?'

'Your mind's a midden. Mrs Harris bin sharing the family tent with my youngsters while I've been sleeping–'

Brookner spat a laugh. 'Ain't been much sleeping had, what with you and her looking so dark around the eyes through lack of it. Put on that neat dress back at the rendez-vous, an' held herself real tall, strutting between the wagons like she was a person, but she's nothing but a cheap–'

Dropping his head, Jed hit Brookner in the midriff while he was still spouting. They tumbled backwards in a heap, their arms locked about each other. Brookner caught Jed a glancing headbutt while Jed piled in a couple of short jabs below the ribs. They wrestled some more and Jed broke the big man's grip, only to be felled by a blow across the back from a rock. He dodged the next, rolling free to jump to his feet.

'Bushwhackers breed bushwhackers. Now I understand why yer offspring don't fight fair.'

Brookner grinned and made a lunge. Jed sidestepped, bringing up his boot into the man's crotch. With a gasp Brookner started to collapse. Jed bunched his fist, slamming the cross down on his jaw with the full weight of his good shoulder behind it.

'You keep yer eyes an' yer mind offa Mrs Harris,' he snarled, but Brookner was beyond comprehending.

Jed and Tom limped back to their wagon. 'Not a word to Mrs Harris,' Jed warned.

'She'll know.'

'Knowin' and being told is two different matters.'

Mrs Harris was at first horrified, then speechless, but it lasted only long enough to bring water and a cloth to make a start on Tom's face. 'Jacob said it was Tom who was fighting. You look as if you joined in, too. What happened?'

Jed drew a breath and felt his ribs burn. 'Men's business.'

Mrs Harris stood upright, but he was ready for that glare of hers and simply glared back. Her gaze slid across his shoulder.

'Well, here comes more *men's business* so you'd better deal with it.' She turned her attention back to Tom. 'Let's get this shirt off and have a look at you.'

There was an entire posse marching up the wagons. Fremont led the way, a woman gesticulating at his side. Jed grimaced when he saw that it was the formidable Mrs Brookner. They came to a halt a few feet from the wagon. Mrs Brookner suffered from the same pointing finger as her husband.

'That man–'

'Enough!' Fremont called. 'Longman, I knew this was–'

Mrs Brookner's scream was deafening, her pointing fingers wavering slightly as her eyes bulged. *'Smallpox!'*

FOUR

'No matter which way this is cut, the blame lies at yer own feet.'

Fremont was scowling down at them from the back of his grey, its hoofs planted a good distance from where Jed and Mrs Harris were standing by the team.

'It ain't smallpox,' Jed stated.

'You some quack doctor to know that, are you? Or are you just going by the fact that your youngest is still breathing?' Fremont stood in his stirrups and glared. 'Or are you going to give me the barefaced lie that you haven't been hiding him away 'cos he's been sick?'

'Tom's rash isn't smallpox, Colonel Fremont.'

'I'll be grateful for you keeping your peace, Mrs Harris. You're not exonerated in any o' this. I knew from the off that having a lone woman along would cause friction, and here we are, not even a month o' Sundays gone and you're showing your heels like a filly in new grass.'

'Watch yer lip,' Jed scolded. 'You're talking to a respectable married woman.'

Fremont huffed some and sat back in his saddle. 'I'm not going down that trail with either of you. The fact is that you, Longman, have gone against the articles you signed by not reporting a sickness.'

'Well I'm reporting it now and I'll take my time in quarantine. But I got eyes, Fremont, and that ain't what's happening here. I've helped my share of wagons across the river with my team, but all I see is us on this side and everyone else on the other. Where's the team to double wi' mine?'

Fremont's gaze slid away and Jed tore off his hat to thump it against his knee. 'Goddamn it, Fremont, you can't abandon us here.'

'No one's abandoning anyone. You've got

six healthy oxen that have been well rested. The water hardly laps the wagon bottom. It'll not cause you a problem.'

'You could have brought your team.'

'Sure I could. And then I'd have had anarchy. Now listen good, Longman. There's more to this than a couple of sick kids. There's a section that's for running you off, even talk of putting a bullet in one o' your lead ox–'

'That's mighty Christian of 'em.'

'Don't get riled. I'm just telling you this so you're certain about the strength of feeling across there. It'll blow over – so long as no one gets sick – and then they'll be bringing you cakes like it's a church social. It's just better for everyone if there's some distance between y'all, understand?' He shifted in his saddle. 'O'course, the option is to go back and wait on other travellers.'

'I ain't turning back.'

A heavy spit of rain darkened the crown of Fremont's hat. Another caught the neck of his horse. Fremont glanced across the water. The lead wagons were pulling out. 'I'll call on you,' he said.

'You do that,' Jed retorted, but the wagon-master was already swinging round his grey, heading for the river.

'Mr Longman…' Mrs Harris drew closer. 'Mr Longman, I have to tell you this. I realize you have need of me with Tom being sick, but my need is to reach my husband. If you decide to turn back–'

'You got cloth ears, woman? This wagon ain't turning back.'

Her cheek caught the slap of a raindrop. She didn't wipe it away, but let it stream like a tear. Her eyes held no pain, though. Her shoulders were squaring even before she lifted her chin.

'Then might I suggest we stop grinding our teeth, unload my mules and harness them in front of the oxen?' She left him to follow in her wake as she strode to the rear of the wagon.

'Those pack-mules ever been in harness?'

'I've no idea,' she snapped. 'Perhaps you

should ask them.'

Baddell pulled down his hat and buttoned his slicker. Others were drawing on theirs as the droplets began to crowd. 'Well?'

McIntyre rose from his haunches, brushing the trail-dirt from his gloves. 'They're racing the river.'

'Don't tell me what I already know. How far ahead are they?'

'I ain't no medicine man. My guess is they're already at the ford. That white hat they got leading 'em seemed to know what he were doin'.'

Baddell spat a string of tobacco juice. 'Then he'll be the first for a bullet.'

'That ain't what we're supposed to be about,' McIntyre countered. 'Soft an' quiet, remember? Just like every other time. We'll have problems enough if the river starts to flood afore we can get the critters back across this side.'

He noticed Golder bringing his horse to stand beside Baddell's. The younger man hadn't said more than a dozen words in his hearing since they'd returned to the sod-house, but his eyes had taken on a squint meaner than a wounded grizzly's.

'Don't worry,' Baddell said in a flat tone. 'You'll get what you want, and we'll take what we want.'

McIntyre wasn't sure he liked the sound of that, even less the glimpse of Golder's sly smile.

The rain came softly at first, as if testing the land, and then the wind took charge and it turned into a regular downpour. The mules didn't take kindly to their makeshift harness. When the brake was released on the wagon and Jed cracked the whip, the ox-team seemed to drive the mules rather than them taking their share of the strain. All that changed when they entered the water. After an initial panic the mules began to swim. Jed was riding Mrs Harris's chestnut, and with shouts and cracks of the whip he got the wagon heading diagonally upstream until near the half-way point, then, with a perturbing slide of wheels, he eased them round. With the current pushing from behind and the far bank growing closer, the mules kicked, the oxen behind them. It seemed in no time at all that the sodden animals were dragging themselves up the muddy incline. Jed kept at them until they'd reached the top before drawing the horse alongside the wagon. The expressions of his children, and of Mrs Harris, caused him to grin.

'You look as if you've been talkin' to St Peter at the Gate. Lost no one, have we? Lost no vittles? Then that makes itself a good crossing.'

On land the mules and oxen didn't get on so well together, so the mules were un-hitched from the team. Jed wouldn't waste time relieving his wagon of Mrs Harris's possessions, though, despite their added weight. He needed to have the other wagons in view before the night stop, even if his was to be quarantined outside their perimeter. It proved a slow business. Softened by the rain, the trail had been churned by the animals ahead of them and Jed took to testing each rutted dip and hollow before being confident of leading his wagon through. Too often another route had to be found. He couldn't chance the wagon being caught in a morass where two mules and a horse might not be enough to help the oxen pull it clear. They'd never catch up if the wagon had to be unloaded to drag it free.

The rain fell relentlessly, the louring clouds bringing on an early night. It was a relief when Jake's sharp eyes picked out the first flicker of a lamp, but that turned to dismay when they realized that the lone lamp was fixed to a stake driven into the ground.

Mrs Harris climbed off the wagon. 'Is this what I think it is?'

'I reckon,' muttered Jed. 'They'll be ahead and this is as close as they want us.'

'Or one of them put this here to make us think that and they have carried on.'

He'd been harbouring the suspicion himself, but it seemed contrary coming from her. He tipped his hat to catch sight of her face and water dribbled off the brim. Her own hat was pressed low on her brow, but it hadn't stopped lanks of wet hair escaping from its crown. The rain was making her skin glisten, and he found his gaze following the tight line of her lips. Rubbing a hand over his stubble, he looked away.

'How are the boys?' He was surprised at the steadiness of his voice.

'Tom won't be doing chores for a few days, but that's due to the beating he received, not the rash. I'll help with the oxen, *after* you check on our neighbours.'

It was almost an order, but Jed didn't argue. He was glad to put some space between them.

The wagons were there, the horses and mules already corralled within the circle. Fremont had been watching for him and met him on the track.

'Pleased to see you made it, Longman.'

67

'Good o' you to wait on us, Colonel.'

'There's no need to be frosty. We've been through this exchange once and I'm not about to have it started over. Everyone's nerves are a little stretched in this wet but it isn't going do us, nor you an' yours, any harm. The bugle will sound at four a.m sharp and I'll personally walk down a ways to ensure you hear it. Now I suggest, like everyone else, you get some vittles and some shut-eye, and let's all hope that come the morrow this rain's played itself out.'

On his return to the wagon Jed found a hatless Mrs Harris, her damp hair twisting free of its loose pins, doling out hard biscuits and jerky to the boys. A steady drip from one of the hazel hoops was being caught in a skillet, and he was uncertain which was the more irritating, the constant dull drumming on the canvas or the pinging in the pan. He waved aside her offer of food and went back out into the rain to tend the animals. Coming up from the creek with laden buckets, he paused at the sight of her.

She was hammering pegs, raising the tents, her short skirt clinging wet to her thighs.

McIntyre sat on the ground, water puddling round his slicker, his hat angled low against the rain. The river had been running fast but was not yet in flood. He hoped it stayed that way until they'd got the critters back across. McIntyre hated this weather, but then so did every man alive, that was why it worked so well for them. Raising his head he glanced about the small groups. No one was saying much, Baddell even less than usual, and that worried him.

'They're back!'

The horses snickered at the sudden stirring of the men as Scholl and Golder appeared over the low rise.

'They're all tucked up, an' just two guards,' announced Scholl. 'One of the wagons is away on its own.'

Golder grinned at Baddell. 'An' guess who it belongs to?'

The group mounted to take the short ride,

the heavy rain muffling every sound. The dirt farmers had even lit lanterns as a beacon to guide them in. Not a man spoke as they fell to the practised drill. McIntyre unwrapped the clutch of arrows tied behind his saddle and dished out two or three to those who came for them. He kept some for himself and strung the short bow. A couple of men had stowed their slickers and were donning painted skin shirts. Golder was stripping to the waist. McIntyre tried not to glance at his expression, but the pull was intense. A man might enjoy his work, but Golder truly revelled in his.

Sallis turned at the sound. A dull thud, he thought, but couldn't be sure. He listened some more, his long-gun at the ready, but the drumming of the rain on tent and wagon canvas was enough to send a man mad. Or make him hear things. It was impossible to see more than a few paces from a lamp. Thompson was out there, circling the tents in the opposite direction, and

Sallis was mindful that he hadn't to spook on seeing his shadow approach.

He was still thinking of Thompson when his head was jerked back and a fire filled his throat; he was still gurgling for a breath when he felt the blade slice his forehead and his hair start to lift.

Jolted awake, Jed flung the quilt from himself in an automatic reaction. Vern, laid in his arms, cried out at the sudden movement. And then Jed heard a shot. He didn't wait for another, but grabbed Vern by the arm and dumped him in the walkway between the packing, to land on top of Tom. In the darkness he reached out to the other side of the wagon until he caught hold of Jake, dragging him over the edge as well. Their assorted shouting and wailing filled the vehicle with cries.

'Quiet, there!'

Another gunshot effected what his own words had not. Like the last, the shot was a distance away. It was the circle under attack, not them. Jed scrambled along the top of the boxes, feeling for his rifle, cursing for not having it within a hand's reach. Finally grasping it, he climbed over the wagon seat out into the rain.

'An' don't you three move from there!'

The thundering he'd taken for the rain on canvas was easier to distinguish out in the wet. The train's oxen were being run off – no, the horses. Goddamn Indians had un-linked the chains and got inside the circle. What were they doin' over there?

He took a step and remembered their own mounts, Mrs Harris's mounts, and he ran between the wagon and the tents shouting her name, coming to a sliding halt at the rear of the wagon. The picket pins were there, a foot or so of tethering line dangling in the mud, but no mounts. Jed swore again and slithered to the fore of the wagon.

'M'Harris!'

The barrels of her scattergun were coming out of her tent, she behind them.

'Injuns!' he rasped. 'Stay wi' the boys an' don't light a lamp.'

He started for the circle, but caught his step after a dozen yards. He could hardly see a hand before him. The beat of hoofs was ebbing, the shots, too. Wherever they were heading, it wasn't towards him. And they'd sniffed round his wagon already, hadn't they, and taken the mules. He looked back, but even at that short distance the canvas of wagon and tents was no more than a faint imprint on the night. Gripping his rifle, he strode out for the circle.

Lamps were lit and more being lit, folks moving in front of them as if they were lining up for a duck shoot. Jed couldn't believe their stupidity. He shouted to warn he was coming in, but with all the hollering going on, and the rain being so heavy, no one took any notice.

'What happened?' he asked as he came upon the nearest wagon.

The man there turned to stare at him with eyes so wide that the whites were showing all around. Brookner had had the scare of his life.

'What the devil do you think happened?' he roared, pointing to an arrow sticking out of the dirt. 'Goddamn Pawnee ran off the herd. Came for scalps, they did. An' took 'em, too! Goddamn heathens should all be burned alive!'

Jed moved between the wagons. Of the corralled animals only two milk-cows and a hobbling mule were left in the circle. At one side someone injured was being tended. Not far away a gaggle of sobbing women were comforting one another. When their skirts moved he caught sight of a man's legs sticking out from beneath a spread blanket. Three horses were led in and tethered to be saddled. Men gathered round, arguing. It was obvious to Jed that they were gearing up for a search party – in the rain and in the dark. He shook his head and moved through the throng.

'Longman!' Fremont hurried across. His clothing was mud-splattered, his white hat missing from his grey hair. 'Good to see you in one piece, Longman. Your wagon hit?'

'Only took the horse and mules. God knows where the oxen be. What happened?'

'Snook up on the guards. Thompson's got his head smashed, Sallis his throat cut. Scalped him, too. I never saw a one, but some are saying it were Kaw, some Pawnee. They're working themselves into a lather here.'

'Looks to me like they're working themselves up to get killed.'

'Longman!' A man in a dark woollen coat was waving a gun at them. 'Get your horse, Longman. We need every man.'

'Ain't got no horse to get,' Jed retorted. 'Wouldn't join yer if I had, neither. You'll not be able to see the trail afore daybreak. Or were yer gonna carry lamps to make it easy for 'em to pick you off?'

The man's expression changed, but Jed didn't wait for his reply, if any was coming. He pushed by Fremont and headed out of the circle.

'Longman, your boys–'

'Injun!'

The cry was taken up and in the panic some dived for cover beneath the wagons, others levelled rifles where they stood. Only one got off a shot before Fremont called to hold fire, running along the line, knocking down the barrels. Jed peered into the rain, at the ghostly figure which had not moved.

'Mrs Harris? Lord, woman! You wanna be shot? Get in here!'

She walked towards them, slow and somehow deliberate. Jed made out the short scattergun held limp in her hand, the mud covering the front of her dress. Hairs began to rise on his neck as he realized the men behind him stood as silent as a host. Shadows danced on the ground in front of him; someone was bringing up a lamp. Despite the rain coursing down her, she was covered in blood. Her face was streaked with it, her clothing overwhelmed by it.

She stopped as if surprised to see them there, her head moving slowly, her gaze resting on an arrow sticking out of the ground.

'They're not Indians,' she said. 'They're white men.'

As a bustling group, they moved down to Longman's wagon. Jed grabbed a lamp from one of the men and called his boys. Tom was sitting in front of his brothers, Mrs Harris's long scattergun held at the ready. She'd been there. Streaks of blood glistened red everywhere she'd touched. He spoke to his boys, calmed them, took the gun from Tom's trembling hand, and went outside.

Someone had dragged the tent from its pegs and they were crowding round staring, all except Brookner, who was spewing up his stomach contents. Jed held his breath against the stench of burst entrails and pushed himself to the fore. The corpse was certainly no Indian, despite his lack of shirt. The shotgun blast, from such a distance and with both barrels, had almost cut him in two. His arms were clean below the elbow. One hand still held a knife.

'Looks like we got ourselves our scalper,' someone intoned.

'Ain't he one of those fellas caught in the flood?'

There was a drone of muttering, and Fremont took his lamp closer to the rain-washed face. 'Goddammit, we fed them fellas.'

Jed went down on his haunches, turning the dead man's face for a better look. He couldn't be sure, he told himself, but knew he was, and he wished he'd taken more notice when the three men had come into their midst.

'Changes things a mite,' Fremont said. 'If white men are riding with Injuns, they'll be Comancheros.'

'They ain't Comancheros,' Jed said. 'Plain ordinary bushwhackers is what they be, just muddying the water with arrows and such.'

Brookner scowled. 'How come you've suddenly got an opinion worth listenin' to?'

''Cos I've run into him afore, back East some ways. He's a road agent.'

'Well, he's a dead road agent now.'

''Tain't him that's the worry. It's his

partner, Baddell.'

As he spoke, as he remembered, Jed felt a familiar gnawing begin in the pit of his stomach. He kept his hat pulled down, not wanting to meet anyone's gaze in case they questioned him, though he couldn't ignore Mrs Harris. She had come closer and was staring at him with that ghost-grey face and that bloodied clothing that the rain refused to wash clean. But he couldn't tell her, not yet.

Without a word he stepped round her to climb the front of the wagon. From the possibles box behind the seat he pulled out the sack carrying the Peacemaker, and began to feed it with lead.

FIVE

'What d'yer mean yer don't know where he is? I left yer holding his horse!'

In the dark and the pouring rain, amid the restless herd of captured animals, Scholl fought to keep his skittish mount facing Baddell.

'You don't understand. They spooked. Golder's tore the rein outta my hand and bolted. I went after it but it got away from me at the creek. By the time I got back to the tent–'

Baddell stood in his stirrups. 'I understand fine. Yer left 'im, yer lily-livered bastard!'

McIntyre pushed his way through to Baddell's side. 'River's running. If we're gonna make this crossing, we're gonna have to make it now.'

'We're going nowhere without Golder.'

'Golder could be anywhere 'tween here and the wagons. Could even have got turned around in the dark.'

Baddell lifted his head. The eye-patch stood out like an open door to Hell in Baddell's rain-washed face and McIntyre knew there'd be no arguing now and breathing later.

'Mac's right,' Scholl said. 'And we've got a whole corral full of critters just waiting to be turned into silver dollars.'

Baddell tore open his slicker. 'You want to cross, then you go get 'em.'

McIntyre didn't see the handgun drawn but the noise of the hammer being thumbed was loud, even in the pounding rain. He tried to pull his mount away, but the animal wouldn't respond. And then the darkness spurted with light and the sound of the shots deadened his hearing. He clung to the wet saddle of his bucking mount and reined in as hard as his numb hands could manage to stop his horse bolting along with the stampeding livestock. Amid the braying and baying he thought he heard a fearful scream, but he reckoned it was only a fancy.

Jed Longman spent a damp night with his sons and Mrs Harris cramped in the loaded wagon. His two youngest whimpered before falling into a fitful sleep. He wouldn't allow a light, and wouldn't hold them in the darkness, needing his arms free to cradle the rifle across his knees and get acquainted, again, with the weight of the Peacemaker. Fremont had dismissed his request to move his family to the main clutch of wagons.

'Those bushwhackers got what they wanted,' the wagonmaster had said. 'They're not coming back tonight or any other night.'

Maybe not that night, but they'd be back, Jed was sure of it. He was sure of Baddell.

The rain slackened to a loose drizzle with the coming of the dawn. Jed eased himself over the tailgate before the others stirred, mindful of how exposed the single wagon stood. There was no cluster of rocks to hide

82

behind, no stand of trees close by to give cover. There were undulating hillocks of pasture, knee-high brush between the wagon and the raging creek, the mired road winding away, but that was it. He scanned the misty landscape while he wondered what options were open to him. Too few, he realized. A man with a rifle could pick him off as he stood there contemplating. But that wouldn't happen. That wasn't Baddell's way. It would be too final, and far, far too fast.

A few paces distant the downed tent lay where it had been thrown over Golder. The man's boots stuck out, one heel pointing skywards, the other foot flat to the ground. Jed set down the rifle and began the grim task of dragging the body into the brush away from the wagon. He didn't want his boys seeing such a sight.

When he returned Mrs Harris was picking through her possessions, scrubbing at each piece with a cloth continuously being rinsed in the pail at her feet. Beside it lay the short scattergun that had done such deadly work the night before.

'Is that cocked?' he asked.

She turned to look at him. It was a relief to see that there was colour in her cheeks once again. She had shed her bloodied clothing in favour of the riding skirt.

'No, it's not cocked. You're safe.'

'But my boys wouldn't have been, would they, if they'd crawled into your tent last night. Who sleeps with a cocked coach-gun beneath their blanket?'

'I do. And even in my sleep, Mr Longman, I know the difference between a boy seeking comfort and a man seeking pleasure.'

They eyed each other for a long moment.

'Something the notable Mr Harris passed on, was it, along with his guns and his horse?'

'Bushcraft. He lectures on it. The Art of Self-Reliance in the Face of Adversity.'

'The *what?*'

'My husband is an Englishman, the sort of Englishman who takes tea at four-thirty and who shoots tigers in India and rhinoceros in Africa. He came to this continent to shoot bear and buffalo.'

'And left you in the States while he did it.'

'His current journey West was on a business venture, Mr Longman, and he left me back East because I was confined with our child. Alas, I miscarried. While I was convalescing his letters stopped. They began arriving again two months ago, requesting funds, but they weren't written in his hand.'

Jed shifted his weight and raised an eyebrow. 'Don't sound like the sort of journey a man would want his wife to make.'

'Perhaps not, but I'm making it all the same. I am, though, somewhat at a loss as to how to proceed without draught animals.'

He lifted his hat and ran his fingers through his hair. 'That might not be the biggest problem. Round up the boys. We're paying the wagons a visit.'

Six men on horseback walked their mounts away from the river in a straggling line, each far enough from the next man so as to see him clearly enough and catch his attention with a signalled hat or a shrill whistle. It wasn't particularly far in the misty drizzle, but Baddell was taking no chances on Golder being passed unnoticed. No one dare mention the possibility that Golder might be wounded. McIntyre hoped that would be the worst of it. If Golder was dead there would be no accounting for what Baddell might do.

It was a good hour before a signal was raised, but by the frantic gestures Castilio was making it wasn't Golder he'd spied. With the horses secured, the men snaked their way to the crest of a knoll to peer down into the flatlands below them. A lone rider was herding a motley group of milk-cows, oxen and mules, about a dozen animals in all, strays from their wild ride the night before. Every so often the man lifted his arm and a moment later a soft crack was carried on the wind.

'Aw, look at the greenhorn,' said Wallace,

peering through a telescope. 'Trying to be a regular range-rider, he is.'

Baddell threw himself down and reached out to jerk the brass instrument from his hand.

'How long you had this?' he demanded, peering through the piece.

Wallace stopped masticating the chewing tobacco bulging against his cheek and stared at Baddell. Easing his position a little, he fired a stream of juice across the sparse grass in front of them.

'Since I traded it for the life of a Yankee officer I got the drop on. Shot him anyway, a neat hole through the forehead. Blew his brains right outta the back o'his skull.'

Baddell lowered the telescope, slowly turning his head until the two men met eye to eye. They hung there a moment neither giving way, then Baddell's face lit, and roaring with laughter he handed back the telescope.

'Then it's yours, won fair an' square!'

Wallace grinned in response, the brown

tobacco juice squeezing between his stained teeth. Baddell clapped him between the shoulders and sprang to his feet. 'Come on, boys. Let's round up this nester and see what he has to say.'

Without a flicker of his exuberant expression he drew his revolver and shot Wallace clean through his hat and the back of his head. Wallace jerked the once and lay still.

'Don't you threaten me, y'cur!' Baddell snarled at the corpse. 'You blew that Yankee's brains outta the back of his head? Well, I just blown yours outta your nose.'

Holstering his gun, he stepped on Wallace's hat. There was a grinding of shattered bone, and blood oozed, thick and dark, from beneath the brim. Reaching down, Baddell dragged the telescope from Wallace's limp fingers, catching his action to turn and stare at his stunned men.

'What you all standing there wide-eyeing me for? 'Cos o' this bastard, that nester's been spooked. Git after him afore he rides off.'

Not a man glanced at another as they made their way down the slope to the horses. Catching the nester was a unifying objective, Wallace a retreating memory.

'That's as far as yer come, Longman.'

Jed put out his hand, but he knew that Mrs Harris had held back the boys as soon as Brookner stepped from the side of the wagon, the rifle half-way to his shoulder. He knew, too, that the most stupid move he had made all year was to put out his right hand, leaving it fanning the air above the Peacemaker. Brookner was slow, had possibly not noticed he was wearing the gun belt, but as sure as breathing he'd notice it as soon as the fanning hand lowered to his side. He didn't trust Brookner to plug him straight, either, even from such a distance. Like as not in his panic he'd take one of his boys by mistake.

An old anger uncurled in Jed's belly, firing up the muscles in his back. His chin lifted, his stance eased. He could see himself doing it, as if he was watching his own reflection in a glass. Martha had been right. He'd always laughed at her belief, but she'd been right all along. When he strapped on the gun, he strapped on the attitude.

Something inside him cringed when the fanning hand lifted some more to remove the hat from his head, but the anger disappeared faster than water down a drain hole. He thought about his boys standing behind him, thought about them real hard, and knew he'd done the right thing.

'I need to speak to Colonel Fremont.'

'No, y'don't. You need to turn tail an' take those stinking kids back to yer wagon afore the good folks here gets their fever. There's been enough burying done today.'

Jed's gaze was roaming over Brookner's shoulder. Where there'd been only a couple of milk-cows and a handful of mounts the previous night, oxen were being tethered to wagon wheels to have their limbs checked. Between the hooped canvas he glimpsed a mule.

'I got information about Baddell he needs to know.'

'Yeah,' said Brookner, the rifle lowering a little as he extended his neck and curled his lip. 'Information like how you knowed that Golder fella was wanted by the law. We been doing some talking about how you knowed that information.' The rifle swept in an arc. 'Move aside there and let them working work.'

Jed glanced behind him. Two tired oxen were being driven towards the wagons by a youth riding a horse bareback.

'Found 'em grazing near the overhang, Mr Brookner. More down there, too. I'll get help and we'll go round 'em up.'

'How many's there?' Jed asked.

'Don't go poking your nose in,' Brookner warned. 'No one's found your animals. You want 'em, you go look for 'em yourself.'

'Boy,' Jed ordered, 'you stay wi' the wagons and don't you leave 'em for yourself.'

The boy pulled a face and mewled something inaudible. Brookner was stepping forward to state his piece again, but Jed ignored them both. He'd seen a white hat pass between the wagons. 'Fremont!'

'Mr Longman, luck's running with us, it seems.' Fremont patted the rump of the ox lumbering past him as he and Moynihan approached.

'Luck, nothing. How easy is the stock being found, Fremont? And how many unarmed youngsters you got out there looking?'

Fremont's expression clouded. Jed watched the wagonmaster glance towards Mrs Harris and his boys. 'Ease your tone, Longman. Things are still tetchy round here, and I don't think–'

'Seems that way to me, too. The wagons are looked over real close to reckon their worth. The stock's run off. But by morning they're just sitting on the land waiting to be slipped back into harness. An' all you can *think* is that luck's running your way.'

'It is,' said Fremont. 'Those road agents miscalculated. It's my guess that the river rose too fast for them to make the crossing.'

'So they just abandoned 'em, did they? After going to all that trouble? Why not move 'em down river some and wait for the waters to recede? We're hardly going to be in hot pursuit, are we, considering they stole the horses, too.'

'So what is it you're saying Longman? Spit it out.'

Jed took a breath and held it. 'Their reason for being here's changed. Golder's dead. Baddell's out for revenge. And he'll take it, too, on anyone he can lay his hands on.'

A rifle-barrel came up against Jed's chest. 'Yeah, we still ain't got to the bottom of how you know so much about these fellas, have we?'

Jed turned to glare at Brookner, then Fremont and his second. 'I know about these fellas,' he snarled, 'because their faces stared out from Wanted posters on my office wall.'

The nester turned out to be a boy with hardly a piece of down on his cheeks to show a razor, but that didn't stop Baddell questioning him with his fist. Every time the boy fell, Girvan was there to pick him up and hold him while Baddell hit him some more. McIntyre stepped from one foot to the other, not wanting to watch but unable to look away. Finally he intervened.

'He ain't gonna tell you nothin' with a broke jaw.'

'The nester ain't gonna tell us nothin' 'cos he don't know nothin' exceptin' that he's a goddamn stinkin' nester!'

Baddell stepped over to the sagging boy and leaned into his bloodied face. 'Gonna cry fer yer momma again, kid?'

McIntyre felt himself turn clammy between the shoulders. 'If Golder's been took–'

Baddell's head shot up, the dark eyepatch holding him firmer than the unblinking eye. 'And why would Golder be took?'

It seemed to McIntyre that there was a

discernible shifting in the stance of the men around him, as if they were giving him space. He fought the urge to lick his drying lips.

'Don't know, rightly. But they'd be sure to keep him safe, like, on account o' needing a trading-piece, as they ain't got no animals to pull them wagons.'

'So...?'

'So...' McIntyre was sweating. It had never been this hard to string settlers a line. '...so we'll need a trading piece to get him back is all I was thinkin'.'

Baddell stared at him a moment before raising himself and giving the boy a half-hearted kick.

'Fix a necktie on this nester and drag him behind a saddle. We're wasting time here when we should be scouting for Golder.' Reaching for his own mount, he called the men to their horses.

There was the striking of a match and the smell of a strong cheroot. A cloud of cloying smoke wafted round McIntyre's head. He peered through it, trying not to let his eyes water. Castilio stood there, grinning.

'To me you never looked a brave man, Señor Mac. You must, then, be *idiota*.'

Fremont was keeping inquisitive ears at a distance, not wanting panic to spread between the wagons at the thought that Baddell's men might be waiting to jump their kin out alone on the prairie. Jed didn't look up much, not wanting to draw attention, but it seemed that Fremont's ploy wasn't being completely successful. Folks knew that something was afoot, especially with Moynihan reporting to him every time someone came in with a few of the strays, and no one being allowed to leave.

Nursing his coffee, Jed mulled over the mess he was making of the whole thing. Mrs Harris and his boys still sat in the dirt outside the wagon's circle, a target for any good rifle, and despite his continued requests the colonel seemed to be in no hurry for an ox team to be sent out to drag his wagon in for safety. There was only so much a man could emphasize without it sounding like begging.

'So ... you were sheriff, eh?'

Jed shook his head. 'Nothin' so fancy. Town deputy for a while. Mostly I regulated for stage and freighting companies. You know how it is, a man gets a hankering to be somebody, to have folks look at him an' that.' He gazed hard at Fremont, standing there in his clean white hat, calling himself colonel, and he tried not to feel bitter.

'I guess that could explain the notches on the butt of your pistol there.'

Jed's palm moved to cover the rosewood handle of the Peacemaker, but he'd realized long ago that the dead men's fingers couldn't be hidden. They only pointed him out for ridicule.

'I guess,' continued Fremont, 'marking the barrel ain't as good. Folks can't see them until the weapon's drawn. There's no mistake when they're sported on the butt. Is there, Mr Longman?'

'Different life, Colonel. Different person.'

'And was it this different person who faced down Baddell and his gang?'

'No one faces down Baddell. That ain't how he works it.'

'Is he, Mr Longman, what you're running away from?'

Jed reined in the anger turning acid in his stomach and lifted his head to stare Fremont square in the eye.

'I ain't running away from nobody. I'm taking my boys to a better life out West. An' I want 'em in the circle, Colonel. I want 'em in the circle right now, fever or no fever. Safety in numbers. That's what I signed the articles fer an' came under yer wing.'

'Of course, Mr Longman. A regulator with a freighting company understands the minds of bushwhackers. We need to talk some more.'

'When my wagon's in the circle and I've fed my boys. There's a sight too much jawing been done already.'

The drizzle abated. Sunlight shot holes through the thinning cloud-cover, blessing patches of land with a golden halo and fixing the colours so bright that a man had to squint just to watch them glow. McIntyre reckoned he could have given a right rousing sermon on the sight had he still packed the minister's weeds, had he not swapped them for a bottle and this road to Hell.

The pressure eased on the back of his saddle as the slack was taken up on the rope turned round the pommel. McIntyre threw back a hand to grasp the youngster's arm before he slipped to his knees and was either choked by the noose or trampled beneath the horse's hoofs. He'd talked to him to start with, urging him to hang on to the bedroll, to lean on the horse and walk with it. He'd even told him that everything was going to work out for him. That was when his words stuck in his craw and he'd taken to musing on his old life. It stopped him thinking about the men he was riding with. It stopped him thinking about Baddell. It stopped him thinking about the demise of Wallace.

They came upon the fast-running creek south of the wagon encampment, and followed it past the rocky overhang where mule and oxen had gathered to graze on the lush grass growing in its shadow. The wary animals backed away, but not a man gave them a look to calculate their worth. As soon as the lone wagon was spied the horses were tethered and the men belly-crawled to a vantage point. Baddell brought out the telescope, but McIntyre didn't need a glass to see that the wagon was deserted, or to notice the crows fluttering away to one side as a four-legged varmint crept into the brush to disturb them. He kept his eyes fixed to the spot, his gut turning hollow as he watched. Baddell must have seen it. Someone must have seen it.

The horses were taken to the wagon and tethered again. Not a man had spoken. Not a man had neared Baddell. He stood alone, a gloved hand resting on the top of the wagon's rear wheel, his head slightly bowed, the brim of his hat hiding his face. A breeze rippled the hooped canvas, eddying a swirl of dust over Baddell's muddy boots. One moment he was still, the next he was striding towards the brush. Then the air was rent by his cry, of anger, of grief, of demons within. On and on it went, rising in pitch until it sounded like a woman's scream, and all the time Baddell was twisting his body, his arms flailing the air and beating into himself, throwing off his hat and tearing at his hair.

When it stopped there was a heartbeat of silence before he began striding back towards them, his face colourless, his one eye staring as blankly as the patch hiding the other. McIntyre held his breath as Baddell bore down on him. He didn't move as the gloved hand grasped the rope and unwound it from the pommel of his saddle. He just allowed the youth to be dragged by the neck towards the wagon, just watched as the rope was flung over its canvas cover.

'Secure that!'

From behind the shoulders of their mounts, the men scurried to do Baddell's bidding. The rope was pulled taut, dragging the youth upright against the wagon's side, lifting him until only the toes of his boots touched the ground, until his fingers clawed at the rope around his throat. McIntyre didn't move as the youth's coat was torn from his arms, as Baddell unlooped the stock whip and made the first strike. Even though they were puffed with bruising and sealed with blood, the youth's eyes bulged, his mouth, too, though hardly a sound came out. Baddell kept on, slow and deliberate, as the youth's knees buckled and his grasping hands fell limp, on and on until his own arm must have given in on him. Breathing hard, he turned to his men, the colour in his face high now, sweat glistening on his brow, his one eye as wide as the grin crossing his face beneath the dark eyepatch.

'Ransack the wagon. See what they got.

Bring me somethin' useful from outta there, somethin' Longman will know is his when I use it against 'im.'

Girvan ran forward to climb the tailgate, the outline of his elbows and head pushing against the inside of the canvas. There was a clattering and a banging, and pans and boxes were thrown out on to the turf. As the wagon rocked, the youth swung on his line, the bloodied face and burst eye turning to McIntyre to stare in silent accusation.

'So what we got in there?' Baddell called.

The reply was muffled but discernible. 'Coffee, bacon an' such…'

Girvan's head appeared above the tailgate, his arm following with a lamp and a rope-wrapped jug. 'We got kerosene.'

Baddel grinned. 'Kerosene is good,' he said. 'Kerosene is very good.'

SIX

Dodd and Whitehorn were purposely ignoring Jed Longman as they goaded the four oxen back along the trail towards his isolated wagon. He had no idea what Colonel Fremont had said, or done, to get the men to aid him. All three had appeared red in the face and square in the shoulder, and only Fremont had looked him in the eye. Dodd and Whitehorn were there under duress, and passing between them was as much muttering and low cursing as there was a flicking of the switch. Jed had insisted a switch be used in place of the usual rawhide whip with its tell-tale crack that carried so easily on the breeze, but his stance had provoked a snarling response from the two men that the Colonel had quashed with a terse word.

Jed didn't care what they thought, or how they acted towards him. Not having to cope with their conversation meant that he could concentrate on the gentle rise and fall of the land either side of the trail, watching for sign of a glint of metal, or a shadow that could not be cast by the short vegetation. He became aware of his fingers unduly tightening around the rifle as he held it ready, and he had to force himself to relax. Thinking how he would have done this back in the old days didn't help. In the old days he would never have led two men into a possible line of fire without any source of cover, not for some sod-buster's wagon, even if it contained all the man owned in the world. And then he saw the smoke.

'Somethin's afire!' called Dodd, standing as still as a fence-post to point at the billowing cloud.

Jumping forward Jed pushed him in the back. 'Get between the ox pairs and keep your heads low!'

Whitehorn dug his heels into the dirt,

trying to halt the heavy animals, but Jed tore the switch from his hand and beat hard on their dung covered flanks. The four beasts jumped forwards, dragging the two men along with them, and soon it wasn't just smoke in the sky they could see, but the burning wagon. Even Jed drew breath at the sight.

'Mother o'God that's Eli Thompson's boy!' Whitehorn cried, and he ducked under the ox chains ready to go to his aid. A quick jab from Jed's rifle-butt dead-legged him.

'Keep down, I tell yer! He's hanging there to get us to break cover. You want to walk around with a hole in yer head?'

'We can't just leave him there!' wailed Dodd.

'We ain't gonna,' Jed muttered.

Leaning against one of the oxen, he rested his elbow on the stout wooden yoke, taking aim between the animal's ears. The shot rang out and the rifle kicked, the ox, too, in its alarm, but Jed was ready for that. His gaze was fixed on the Thompson boy, and when the youth fell forward trailing a length of rope from his neck, Jed's heart leapt in response.

Whitehorn started to scramble towards the boy but was cowed by Jed's cursed order.

'But he'll burn!'

'He ain't burning,' Jed snapped back, and the realization that he wasn't pulled Jed up short.

The boy was smouldering somewhat, wisps of smoke lifting from his hair and the bundle of rags that seemed to clothe him, but he wasn't alight. Close to his feet stood the pail that Mrs Harris had been using that morning, yet Jed felt sure that she had hung it back on its hook at the rear of the wagon. His family's possessions lay near the tail-gate, scattered where they had been thrown, but the pail had not been tossed in a fit of temper. It stood upright as if it had been set down on purpose after a chore was completed. Had a pail of creek water been thrown over the boy before the wagon had been fired? Had one been thrown over the oiled wagon-canvas? Or was it still sodden from the night's rain, causing more smoke than flame?

'Are we gonna wait until the boy dies or are we gonna do somethin'?' Dodd demanded.

'Wait there,' Jed told them.

Gripping the rifle, he set off in a hunched run, zigzagging across the undulating ground in a wide arc round the wagon, setting himself up as a target as he tried to flush a move from Baddell's gang, but not a shot was fired. Skirting the rear of the wagon and the brush where Golder's body lay hidden, he headed towards the dip holding the fast running creek. To his astonishment he saw Mrs Harris's chestnut feeding there, saddled and ready to ride. When he saw that it was tethered to a peg he hit the ground, rolling himself into a sandy delve. There was no following gunshot, no sarcastic calling. He lay there breathing hard, wondering what in tarnation was going on.

'Longman!'

It wasn't a call for help, but a call to catch his attention, and by its clarity Dodd had ignored his instruction not to move. Sure enough, on finishing his circuit Jed found the two of them next to the wagon, bending over the Thompson boy. Whitehorn's face was as pale as a shroud.

'They've beat him to a pulp an' whipped him raw. Who'd do such a thing? An' to a defenceless boy?'

Jed knew well enough. 'Is he still alive?'

'I guess. He moaned some, but it sounded close to a death rattle to me.'

'Well quit talkin' and get the ox team hitched, then we can put him in the wagon and get him help.'

'Riders!'

Bringing the rifle to his shoulder, Jed took a breath and held it as he sighted down the barrel, but it wasn't Baddell or his gang bearing down on them. It was Colonel Fremont and a party of men from the wagons.

'Took 'em long enough,' Jed muttered. He

cursed as Dodd set off to meet them, hitching the ox team forgotten.

Jed took the pail to the creek and returned to dowse the wagon and its canvas. The fire was all smoke now and no flame at all, so he left it to smoulder and searched the ground round the wagon before there was any more trampling of sign. Horse tracks were numerous in the rain-softened turf, but it was difficult to determine how many mounts had caused them and when. He found a few cigarette-butts and an evil-smelling stub of a cheroot that could have only come from a long way south. If Baddell had spent the last months in Mexico it could account for his silence. But what calibre of desperado had he brought back with him?

There were the fixings of a meal made from Jed's provisions abandoned round a dead fire. One of the skillets had a hole burned nearly through the base. They'd been there that long, at least. Had that been before the Thompson boy was whipped, or had they done the deed and then prepared the vittles, leaving him hanging there? And what had been discussed?

He moved to the boy, still lying on his stomach as he'd fallen. The rope had been cut from his neck, the weals below his jaw showing thick and ugly. Jed didn't lift the stained rags of his shirt. It was plain how bad his back was. Instead he pushed his fingers gently against the boy's armpits, beneath his belt and around his butt. His clothing was damp, and it wasn't from sweat. Jed's blood ran cold. His first notion had been correct. They were sitting in a trap.

A shadow crossed the boy and Jed raised his head, half the first word of warning out before the boot in his ribs robbed him of his breath and catapulted him backwards.

'Get away from him, yer varmint! It's 'cos o' you an' that whore o'yours that all this has happened. Wait 'til Eli gets a hold o' yer.'

'Stop that immediately!' Fremont strode up to bat at the man with his hat. 'Infighting gets us nowhere.' He planted the white hat firmly back on his head and took command.

'Dodd, get done the job you were sent here to do, and hitch up those animals. You two men collect what you can of Longman's possessions there, and toss them into the back o'the wagon.'

Jed hugged his ribs until the initial pain subsided and he could breathe properly again. Reaching out for his dropped rifle to use it as a crutch, he clambered to his feet. 'Fremont—'

'Whitehorn, find a blanket and you men lift the boy into it and get into the wagon.'

'We've been duped, Fremont. The boy's only alive 'cos he's bait Baddell's scheming—'

'Fire!'

Everyone stared at the smoke rising in the distance, gunshots plainly carrying from the circle of wagons. Jed scanned the group around him, counting how many men had been drawn away from the women and children. The colonel lifted his arm to call an order and caught a bullet in the centre of his forehead. He fell in front of Jed, tipping back in a line from his heels, a look of surprise etched into his face. The white hat, now with a small hole above the brim, stayed on his head until he hit the ground then rolled beneath the wagon. Jed followed it, leaving the Thompson boy in the open as men ran in all directions, desperately seeking cover that did not exist.

The first to make his horse died when his head exploded, covering those around him in gore and setting up a fearful screaming among both men and horses. Whitehorn fell at the top of the bank leading to the creek, his chest seeming to erupt in front of him before he toppled out of Jed's sight. Gunfire was returned from those who had thrown themselves into the dirt, but Jed doubted that a single one was aimed at a true target. Wasting ammunition was merely playing into Baddell's hands.

The wagon strained above Jed's head. He felt pressure on his boot and dragged aside his foot as the wheels gave an eighth turn and rocked back into the groove the wagon's weight had created. Twisting in the narrow space, Jed caught sight of the ox team, their legs in agitated movement as their alarm grew. Their harness was hooked to the shaft. The brake was all that was holding the wagon.

He looked about him. The only man close by was the Thompson boy. Jed wondered whether he was still alive and cursed himself for the thought. What if it had been his own eldest?

Leaving his rifle, he crawled a couple of yards from his cover and grabbed the boy's ankles, dragging him back between the wheels. The youth never made a murmur, even when the buffeting reopened the wounds on his face. Jed watched his blood run a little. Blood never ran from a corpse, so he took it to be a good sign. The boy's skin was clammy to the touch but wasn't truly cold. Jed wished he had a canteen to wet his split and blood encrusted lips, but if he'd survived this long he'd manage a little longer.

Jed waited for tell-tale bullet hits to give a notion of where the bushwhackers were hiding, but it seemed that the shooting was coming from only the men around him.

'Hold yer fire!'

He had to call twice more before the intermittent gunshots ceased. He lay in a silence so complete that he could feel his heart beating in his chest and hear the creek rushing past beyond the bank.

'We have to get back to the wagons!' someone shouted. 'I can still hear gunfire from over there. They need us.'

Men rose to a crouching position, heading for scattered horses or the minimal cover the creek offered. Jed pulled the Thompson boy from under the wagon and slung him across one shoulder to clamber up the front wheel and on to the seat. Even before he'd laid the boy down he was kicking free the brake. Beside the footrest sat his son's bag of pebbles. Jed grabbed a handful and threw them at the team, roaring as loudly as he could manage. There was an initial jolt as the oxen took the strain. The wheels turned, riding up out of their worn grooves, and the wagon began to move. Jed felt like hollering in triumph. The animals would drag the wagon any way they saw fit if he wasn't at their head leading them, but he knew he had time to lift the boy over the seat and into the back.

Grasping the boy's wrist he placed a boot on the seat beside him. He heard the report, though the jarring was so severe and came so close behind that he thought he'd been hit. Dropping the boy, he reached out for the hooped canvas to control his fall, but he'd already gone too far and the ground rushed up to meet him, the impact sending a pain searing through his shoulder. His legs seemed to follow him, twisting his body on the ground until he came eye to eye with an ox felled by the single bullet. As it breathed its last the front animals stamped and bellowed in fear, trying to heave the wagon and their dead companion as its fallen partner pawed the ground and the air in turn, snuffling and screaming, trapped at a skewed angle in its half of the double yoke.

Jed struggled clear and looked around for help, but only the dead lay in his field of vision. There wasn't a living man to be seen.

His shoulder was paining him, sewing-pins stabbing into his wrist and fingers. He tried to knead his shoulder and arm as he wondered what to do, but it gave no relief. The crying ox would have to be left to exhaust itself. He dare not risk trying to release it in case he caught a bullet. He wasn't even sure he could release it one-handed. Sweat was beginning to pour from him, to drizzle from his brow and cheeks into his stubble. He was starting to feel light-headed and wanted a drink. He considered trying for the bank and slipping down to the creek, and that was when he remembered Mrs Harris's chestnut. Would it still be tethered there?

Crawling to the bank, he rolled over the edge. It didn't do his shoulder a mite of good, but it didn't garner him a bullet, either, so the trade-off seemed fair. Crouching to keep his head below the flatland above him, he made his way downstream. The chestnut was still there, straining against its tether to nibble at better grass, just as cool as Mrs Harris herself. Jed didn't want to startle it into giving away his position so he clicked his tongue to catch its attention. Its ears pricked, its deep brown eyes swivelling in their sockets as it regarded him. Goddamn, it could even peer at him the way she did.

The chestnut put up no resistance as he led it through the shallows and up the bank to the lee of the wagon. It was perturbed by the bellowing of the oxen and the shaking of the wagon, but it allowed itself to be tied to a wheel. Jed kept up a quiet murmuring as he pulled his pocket-knife and fought to open a blade. A little sawing had the rope cut that held the canvas taut to the wagon's side, and stepping onto the wheel-hub he slipped into the relative shelter of his rig.

Crates and barrels had been upturned or

their lids caved in, but he didn't pause to inspect the damage. The Thompson boy was half over the seat's back rest and within easy reach. If the wagon was being watched, the shuddering caused by the oxen would hide Jed's clumsy movements. He could only hope that no one noticed the boy's legs disappearing inside.

It was more difficult than he had imagined to handle him the two steps to the lifted canvas. Waves of pain coursed down his ribs and up his neck as he struggled to get the boy to the waiting horse, but he managed it, managed to get himself over the wagon's side and back onto his feet, managed to lead the animal down the slope to the creek without the boy's limp body slipping from the saddle.

Through the rushes and water and ankle-deep mud, he kept putting one boot in front of the other, guiding the horse and its precious cargo along the twisting course. It should not have taken long but it seemed to take for ever, and then a whiff of smoke caught in his nostrils, in the horse's, too, for it whinnied. Coming round a bend Jed could see a line of people, women mostly, passing buckets up the bank. There was a shout, and a crack, and something slapped the water to the side of him, but he didn't pause, just kept on walking. He was nearly there, nearly there. He heard Jake's voice, and saw his youngest boys running towards him, Mrs Harris, too. One moment he was smiling at them, the next he was on his knees leaning into her arms. He blinked some, not sure what had happened.

'The boy,' he said. 'The boy's hurt.'

Men were passing him, going towards the horse. He grunted as Mrs Harris patted him on the shoulder, and he eased himself round to see. Eli Thompson had his son in his arms, tears rolling down his cheeks. The bulk of Brookner peeled away from the group to come and stand over Jed.

'The boy,' he spat venomously, 'is dead.'

SEVEN

'Will Pa be OK, Mrs Harris?'

Mrs Harris eyed Jake, his little face pinched with concern, and then she eyed his father, stripped to the waist leaning against a wagon wheel, his body beginning to blossom in bruises. With a cloth soaked in salted water, she dabbed at grazes beside his limp arm, noting the small, stitch-marked scars on his chest and his back. One bullet had gone through clean, the other had rested in the muscle. She eyed him again, and put the past behind. It was his utter dejection that was cause for concern at the moment.

'Your pa will be just fine. He needs a little rest, that's all, then he'll be himself again. Ask Thomas for a piece of jerky from the pack, and a piece for Vernon. The sun is growing low and we'll not be eating round a fire tonight.' She watched him skip away, the afternoon's panic already forgotten.

'They're sound boys, Mr Longman, but they need their father.'

'Won't do 'em no good. Couldn't save the Thompson boy–'

'I didn't see any other man trying.'

'–couldn't save Martha.'

She wondered whether to press him on that, but as if he realized what he'd said, his spine straightened and his head came up to gaze around him. She knew what he was looking at. One wagon's canvas was gone completely, three others a partial loss. One wagon was lying on its side, two wheels smashed beyond repair, another hardly more than a charred skeleton.

'From what everyone is saying it sounds as if it was almost a re-run of last night, except that the riders came in low and fast, whirling pots filled with something flammable and plugged with burning cloth.'

From her pocket she offered him a scorched piece of quilting, crumbling to ash along one side where it had burned. It still smelled of kerosene, except sweeter. He clutched it in his fist, his voice becoming thick.

'Martha spent all winter making this. Wanted a real nice house, she did, with curtains at the windows. She wanted to live in town.'

Mrs Harris bent to wring out the cloth, giving him time. 'They rode off just as fast as they'd come in with not a shot being fired.'

Jed sighed, catching himself. 'Yeah, I know ... until the first man went to put out the flames on his wagon.'

'It was Eli Thompson's brother, and he was dead before he hit the ground.'

'Oh God...'

'Three others went down, all dead, but that wasn't the worst of it. Someone called for the women to take the children to the creek for safety...'

He covered his eyes and winced 'How many?'

'Just Mary Bickersley. We had to listen to her screaming, even after they got her back to the wagons, but she's been quiet for a while now so I think someone's given her a good dose of laudanum.' She looked at him again. 'Was it chance that the men were killed clean and the woman was gut-shot?'

'No.'

She nodded. 'One child caught a broken leg in the crush, and there are a few sprains, I hear. Not to mention you, of course. You've dislocated your shoulder.'

'Figured that.'

'Well, there's no point talking about it. Slot your other arm through the spokes behind you and take a firm hold.'

His expression filled with surprise. 'Something else the redoubtable Mr Harris teaches in his *Art of Self Reliance?*'

'No, my father was a bone-setter. My mother helped him and I learned at her side.'

He did as he was told and she lifted his arm as gently as she could until it was out horizontal to his shoulder. Already he was turning pale, sweat beading on his forehead.

'Do you want a strap to bite on?'

'Nope.'

'If you vomit, mind not to vomit on my shoes.'

'Mrs Harris, I wouldn't d–'

She braced her foot in his armpit before he stopped speaking and tugged with all her strength on his arm. The shoulder gave easier than she expected.

'Not the first time you've sprung that joint, is it?'

She went to fetch a ladle of drinking water. By the time she returned he was rolling his shoulder and clenching his fist. She passed him his shirt.

'Where did you find my horse? And saddled, too?'

'Yeah,' sneered a gritty voice behind them. 'That's one o' the things we'd like to know.'

Mrs Harris moved aside, signalling for the boys to come close. Jed Longman fastened the final button on his shirt and stood to face the crowding deputation.

Moynihan was at the front, though it seemed to Jed that he was being pushed rather than leading it. Tight into his shoulder was the overbearing Brookner, rolling his weight and his menace from one foot to the other. Jed ignored him and looked directly at Moynihan.

'Sorry about the colonel. The two o'yer were close, I know, but I hope me and you can work together on this like–'

'Don't give us any o' this *work together,*' Brookner spat. 'It stinks like the ox-dung it is. The colonel getting his head blowed off is all part o' yer scheme.' He turned to those standing behind him. 'Didn't one o' yer say that it were Longman pointing Fremont out to the shooter?' Swinging round, he stabbed his finger at Jed. 'You're working with 'em, like I allus said, leading men away from these good folks's wagons to halve their protection.'

'I led nobody,' Jed countered. 'Three men takin' out a team to bring in a wagon that should never have been out there in the first place, doesn't constitute halving our protection. It was the smoke that brought Fremont out with a posse, not me.'

'It were her!' cried one of the men.

'Yeah,' snarled Brookner, shooting a glare towards Mrs Harris. 'Flapping an' a-following him about, pecking at him 'til he forced good men to go out there to be gunned down.' He looked over his shoulder. 'Good men,' he repeated. Those behind him trod dirt like milling cattle as they raised their agreement. Brookner rounded back on Jed.

'An' you comes in with yer horse, saddled all neat, like, but no rifle, we see. Y'went out with one, so where is it? Left it for them bushwhackers, didn't yer, to increase their fire-power.'

'I brought back Eli Thompson's boy.'

'Yer brought back a cold corpse, an' not a shot fired in his defence, ain't that right?' The men behind him edged closer, their muttered accusations building.

Jed looked at Moynihan to call some sort of order, but all Moynihan did was give a vague shrug of his shoulders and stutter down his chin. As Jed feared, he was on his own. And if he was on his own, just like in the old days, he was going to have to act, and act big.

He raised his head and glared at the milling group in front of him. 'Enough of this!'

Sweeping his arm across himself in dismissal he took a step towards the men. Moynihan flinched, but Brookner stood his ground. The men behind seemed surprised, and it was to them that Jed addressed himself.

'Enough o' this brawling an' whining an' hiding behind each others' hats. Get out in a line here so I can see you all eye to eye an' let's get a plan of action beat out. Moynihan, how many guards you got posted?'

As he'd expected, Moynihan looked askance. Irritably, Jed gestured him across and like a new-born calf he stumbled to Jed's side. Jed felt a rush of relief, but was careful not to let it show.

'Goddamn it, Moynihan, you think they ain't gonna come back?'

'Well, you'd know that, wouldn't yer?' stormed Brookner as the men around him gradually shuffled into an untidy line. His face began to pink, his gaze flitting left and right as he realized that he'd been isolated. Moynihan, too, backed a pace behind Jed's shoulder, grateful for someone relieving him of the strain of command.

'Yeah, I'd know that,' Jed spat back, 'just like I'd know that you all used half the ammunition you're carrying shooting at blank sky instead of a target. You ask me if I fired my rifle? Well, I'll ask you how many shots were fired by Baddell's men?'

Glaring at Brookner to stare him down, he kept his voice loud so none of the other men would mistake his wrath, and he began to walk the ragged line as if he were inspecting it.

'I'll tell yer how many shots were fired by

129

Baddell's gang. As many as the men who fell, an' the lady. An' don't go thinkin' that were bad-luck shootin', 'cos it were meant. Baddell's a marksman, an' I ain't talkin' about no fancy circus tricks. He was trained in the war to be a sniper.'

'For the goddamn Yankees, I'll wager,' someone called back.

'Don't matter which side trained him. He carried his guns for whatever group o' cutthroats was likely to gain him the biggest booty, an' he set up a ready buyer south o'the Rio Grande for all he could get. By the time the war finished he'd got hisself his own marauders. That's why he works it like a military operation. Sends scouts in first to read the strength of opposition. Comes in quiet in the dead o'night. Hits quick in daylight to draw fire while he has marksmen waiting to pick a kill. Tactics, that's what he uses. Tactics meant to horrify so his victims act without thinkin'. Well, we ain't gonna act like victims. We're gonna start thinkin'. Thinking is gonna be the only way to beat him, the only way. 'Cos there's one thing I can promise yer, he ain't gonna leave us be.'

When Jed paused for breath he realized that he'd worked himself into a regular lather, but looking at the hangdog expressions facing him it seemed that he'd played the right hand. Even Brookner had melted into the line. From behind him Moynihan, too, was finding an authoritative voice.

'Colonel Fremont, he told me how Mr Longman here was a US marshal on the trail of the Baddell gang.'

Jed felt the hairs rise on his neck as a breeze of anxious whispering swept through the line and among the knots of people standing in the shadow of their wagons.

'That were a long time ago,' Jed countered, 'afore Baddell went south to lie low in Mexico. This is here an' now, an' the first thing we needs is to have some figuring on how many men he's got with him. So listen up! How many riders came tossing fire?'

There was a shuffling of feet. One man half-heartedly stepped forward.

'I saw two. They came in close on one another's heels.'

'Two?' another cried behind him. 'We got five burnt wagons, one of 'em down to the axles!'

Jed called for quiet before things got out of hand again. 'Two men would do it if they were carrying more than one apiece. By the looks, three strikes were made to the outside of the wagons, and one went direct inside. That last wagon got its canvas splattered in the mayhem, that's why it ain't got so much damage.'

'Damage? Goddamn, Longman. I've seen kerosene fires afore, but nothing like this.'

'Sure you have, but they been accidents. You ain't never seen kerosene sweetened with sugar and tossed to be lit. Sticks like hoof-glue. Now what about the shooters? How fast did the men try to douse the fires? At once?' He was answered by mutters and nods. 'Then the riders couldn't have been the shooters. So how many shooters?'

There was so much cross-talking and

arguing that Jed wished he'd not asked the question, but to him it sounded as if there were at least another two, maybe three, plus one other across the creek.

'That's six,' said Dodd. 'But what about those at your wagon? How many were there waiting to pick us off? I saw the colonel shot clean not a pace from me. I also saw Fletcher get hit. His head exploded.'

There were gasps from the line, more than one of the women listening gave a cry. Members of Fletcher's family set up a cater-wauling that no amount of comforting from others seemed to lessen.

Jed held up his hand, but even so he had to raise his voice again to be heard. 'I told yer, tactics to horrify. They ain't averse to notching their ammunition. So nobody plays hero. Keep your heads down, an' if you got extra guns arm your womenfolk. Mrs Harris, here, has a scattergun, an' that's ideal.'

As he was talking he swung round to point to her. He never expected to see her holding the coach-gun against her leg, the folds of her skirt hiding its barrel. Even so close it was difficult to tell whether or not it was cocked. He wasn't sure that he wanted to know. To cover his hesitation, he called Moynihan forward.

'We need guards posting, and water bringing in, and all cooking fires to be extinguished by twilight. There are to be no lanterns tonight.' He turned to the men and their gathered families. 'Everyone got that? There will be no lights showing.'

'No lights, eh?' Baddell carried on whittling the stick into a point.

'That's what the man said.' Scholl had his sleeve rolled up and was inspecting scratches and scrapes collected during the long squirm to get him close to the wagons. 'Taking it all real serious they are, too, on account o' him being a US marshal an' all.'

Baddell rocked back his head and laughed aloud. 'Better than a circus act.'

Girvan giggled some and glanced at the

others. 'You saying that he ain't no marshal?'

'Don't worry, boy,' McIntyre intoned, 'you'll see one soon enough, an' from there on in it's a fast trip to a rope.'

Baddell stayed the knife against the wood he was holding. 'Is that dissension I'm hearing from you across there?'

'Just the truth, Baddell, just the truth. Folks get robbed real easy passing through these parts. There's no one here to turn a hair when they lose their horses or cattle. By the time they get anywhere with folks to moan to, everyone figures it's too late to act. But burning out wagons and torturing kids, that's the sort o' thing that rests in the mind an' don't slip out. Shootin' women for the hell o' it...'

Castilio lifted his arms as if holding a gun and fired off an imaginary round. 'Screamed like a stuck pig.'

Baddell saluted him with his knife. 'Wish I'd been there, but I had a delight all o' my own to attend to.' He cupped his hands as if grasping a small ball, and then exploded it in a spray of saliva.

Everyone but McIntyre laughed. He couldn't get the woman's screaming out of his head, nor the sight of the boy dangling by the neck. Their laughter faded and Baddell pointed the knife.

'What you're forgetting, McIntyre, is that a rope fits as neatly for stealing horses and cattle, so the way I sees it a man might as well enjoy himself while he has time.'

'But they're expecting us, Baddell. Seems to me that if they're expecting us, and they ain't got no lights showin', we ain't gonna have surprise working for us no more. An' there's a lot more o' them than there are o' us.'

'That's all that's worrying you, McIntyre? That we're outnumbered? Ha! You ain't figuring on our partners.' Baddell slipped the stick behind his belt and the knife in its sheath, and clambered to his feet.

'Come on, now, boys. Let's get saddled. We need to meet up with 'em an' have a huddle afore night falls. Scholl, you ride

136

with me. I wanna hear more about this loudmouth that's poisoning the water for our friend the marshal back there.'

EIGHT

Jed kept everyone busy, including Moynihan, who was certainly an able second. He found that it was also good to have a buffer between himself and the other travellers. No one wanted to speak to him as one man should to another, preferring to avert their gaze and mutter behind the down-turned brim of a hat. As a group they seemed to think that their problem had a simple solution, and if that solution was found and applied the problem would surely disappear. To their way of thinking Jed was complicating matters, and they weren't convinced that he wasn't doing it for his own ends. Brookner's attitude simply fuelled their resentment. The sense that they should stand together against a common enemy was strangely lacking, and it unnerved Jed.

He instructed Moynihan to keep an open ear, which the man agreed to do so readily that Jed was left wondering if Colonel Fremont had harboured the same misgivings about the company which had signed with him.

Jed turned over in his mind all he knew about Baddell. He tried to look upon the wagons as Baddell would, think as Baddell did. But Jed shied away from that. It was impossible to think as Baddell did. Impossible. He didn't even want to try.

Instead he attempted to organize the travellers as if assembling a huge posse that could not be split. Weapons were checked and an inventory taken of spare ammunition. Half was put aside, half made ready in case it was needed.

'Fire only at what you can see!' he warned.

Barricades were thrown up between the wagons, and men allotted sentry points in threes: one to guard while two slept, though Jed doubted if anyone would. He had all animals both hobbled and contained inside a rope corral set within the confines of the wagon's circle. Baddell's men could be kept out, but if the cattle and mules were spooked it would be like having bullets ricocheting inside a drum.

'Aye,' grumbled the surly Brookner, 'an' if they do spook, trussed like turkeys they'll break legs an' then what use will they be for pulling wagons?'

Jed didn't reply. Did the man prefer his children to be trampled to death?

'It strikes me,' murmured Mrs Harris, 'that it would be better for us all if he were both gagged and bound hand and foot.'

'I'm sorely tempted,' Jed answered, 'but we need his gun.'

'That depends where it's pointed,' she said.

He smiled at her. 'Just so long as you have yours, I won't go worryin' over it. You'd better bed the boys down. Got quilts enough?'

'Oh yes. Mr Moynihan has been very forthcoming with the late colonel's possessions.'

The sunset was as pretty as Jed had ever seen it, wispy clouds turning pink and then scarlet before fading as if embers of a dying fire. He wondered if it was an omen for their salvation, and then fretted in case it was the last sunset he ever saw. Who would take care of his boys if he were gone? He turned to look for them, for Mrs Harris to speak to her, but shapes were merging in the gloom. No one had lit a lamp. He smiled in relief. Despite their griping they were heeding his instructions. If everyone kept still and quiet as he had cautioned perhaps the night would hide them. If the moon didn't rise. If Baddell had become complacent and not left a spotter.

He should have asked Mrs Harris if the wagon-master had bequeathed an extra rifle among his possessions, but without light to see by a rifle only felt good in its weight. In the darkness a handgun and a fast reaction was what determined the measure of a man. He slid his palm over the rosewood handle of the Peacemaker at his hip, feeling the dead men's fingers scrape across his skin, and hoped that he still had what it took, and wasn't just deceiving himself.

The first guard passed without incident. Shuffling and coughing had dropped to a minimum and Jed could even hear the occasional grunt and snore. He hoped it wasn't coming from the sentries. And then a whispering started up to rush around the circle. People began to move, Jed included.

'Hold your places!' he hissed. 'It could be a decoy!'

Every man he went to pointed to another, until at last he found the source of the commotion. Moynihan was already there with a cluster of men peering over the barricade, his rifle ready.

'Mr Gunstead, here, thinks he saw somethin'.'

'Saw something? Saw what?'

'If I knowed, I'd be tellin' yer,' muttered the man at Jed's elbow.'

'Well, where did you see it?'

142

The man made a gesture which could have taken in half the prairie, and Jed had to bite his lip to hold on to his temper.

'There!' said another man. 'A flash!'

Jed could see nothing, and then everyone heard the scream. It sounded so human that Gunstead started chanting a rosary prayer until Jed cuffed him across the shoulder.

'That's an animal,' he said. 'They're doing something to one of the critters out there.'

He turned towards the circle to shout a warning, but caught the first flicker of light in the corner of his eye. Bundles of flame were headed towards the wagons, bouncing across the undulating landscape. He thought horses or mules were dragging lighted brush, and then he realized that the animals, themselves, were alight. The Peacemaker was in his hand, but it was useless at that distance.

'Bring 'em down! Bring 'em down!'

Rifles all around him opened up, and the pitiful creatures started to fall. Jed breathed again, and was immediately caught in the face by spells of wood erupting from the

143

wagon's facia.

'Goddamn it!' yelled Moynihan. 'Someone out there's shootin' at us!'

By the time Jed had wiped the blood from his eyes the men beside him were crouching behind the barricade, a volley of shots ripping through canvas and wood above their heads.

'Hell's teeth! They got a Gatlin' out there?'

Horror swept through the group and eddied along the line of families cowering beside the wagons.

'No! No, they ain't got no Gatlin',' Jed retorted, desperate not to let panic take a hold. 'They'd have used it by now if–' He found himself shouting into the quiet night, and eased his throat. 'They were firing at our muzzle-flashes.'

'What we supposed to throw at 'em, then? Rocks?'

'Keep a watch! It ain't over yet. Moynihan, report any injured and have a check made on the animals. We don't want 'em getting loose.'

'That peppered 'em up a bit,' Baddell said.

McIntyre could see only his shape in the darkness, but the man's smile was evident in the tone of his voice.

'Waste of good animals,' he murmured.

'That you moaning again, McIntyre? Sound like an old Mex washerwoman.'

There was a rumble of laughter in the gloom, Girvan's a higher pitch than the rest. McIntyre could imagine them sat astride their mounts grinning because they didn't know what else to do.

'Some o' them old Mex washerwomen do mighty fine work. They might moan a lot but a man can count on them, not like those simpering hussies in a cantina who hang on your every word.'

A silence reflected back at him, but it wasn't as awesome as McIntyre had expected. Doubtless a muzzle-flash would come from any direction now, not just from Baddell's gun. Or maybe not. They grinned on his command so they'd only shoot on his command. McIntyre sat taller in his saddle. Besides, he mused, he felt better in himself for saying it, much better.

'So why are we sitting here, jawing?' he demanded. 'We got cattle waiting on us back at the stead, and I see more of a percentage in them than I do playing cat and mouse here. If we're doing this, let's do it and get it over with.'

'Quiet down!' Jed called again. His voice was growing hoarse and he could feel himself beginning to lose control of the encampment. 'There'll be a follow-up and we need to hear it coming!'

His boys were wrapped in quilts, hunkered down against a wagon's wheel, Mrs Harris at his shoulder. He could see no more than her outline, but he could smell her womanly scents of soap and food, and he felt comforted by her being there, so strong, so silent, so unlike some of the other women, and far too many of the men.

He returned to keeping watch, but there

was nothing to see. He had hoped for a cloudy night to hide the moon and give them cover, but he was ruing his wish now that it had been granted. A little starlight would put some perspective on their surroundings.

There was movement behind him. He felt Mrs Harris alter her footing. The animals in the rope corral moved again. Jed peered their way, even though he could hardly make out their shapes. A horse whinnied, and he felt a pressure on his arm, slight but positive.

'Jed...'

Then he heard growling, like thunder in hills far off, and sweat stood out on his skin.

'Stampede!'

Gun-flashes lit the night beyond the wagons, shots tearing into Jed's hearing moments later. Baddell's men had rounded up their animals and were running them towards the circle. How many were there? What damage would they do? There was screaming behind him, of women, of animals trapped in their hobbles, desperate to escape.

'Where they headed? Where they headed?' Jed ran along the line. 'Who sees them? Who sees them?'

In the confusion people were bumping into one another. To his left someone was lighting a lamp.

'When you see them bring them down! Bring them down!'

He felt as though he were shouting into the wind with no one hearing him, no one understanding. And then he heard Brookner bellowing above the confusion countermanding his order, calling for no one to shoot. But it was all too late, for the animals were upon them, pans and pails jiggling on their hooks hanging from the wagons. Jed looked for his boys, for Mrs Harris, but he was all turned around and had no idea whose wagon he leaned against.

The thud was loud enough to be caught over the screaming of people and cattle. Wood was splintering, smaller thuds echoing all around, the canvas above him shuddering as if a leafy tree in a strong wind. He fought to recognize a new noise, and then a lamp was being brought forward. Another spluttered into life close by, and he realized what the noise was. A wagon was being pushed sideways on its wheels.

He started to run, looking for it, saw it, its wheel bending against the axle-pin, pushing up turf as if a plough. He opened his mouth to shout a warning and the wagon beside him was jarred and heaved up on to two wheels. A horse jumped the barricade, hitting a man with its fetlock, sending him spinning away, arms flailing. The horse, wide-eyed and snorting, ran on bringing down the rope corral and felling the hobbled animals inside. Another followed it, up over the barricade. An ox tried to match its stride, failing and locking its horns in the barrels and poles, sending up a fearful bawling as it was crushed from behind.

And then the wagon gave a sickening creak and Jed leapt for any space that wasn't beneath it as it toppled. Someone tripped over him as he lay sprawled, another kicked him as he passed, reawakening a multitude of aches and bruises he'd pushed to the back of his mind. Lamps were being lit on every side now, scaring frightened animals further. Women were crying, children screaming, dazed stock limping away from a screeching mule lying with a broken leg and a ruptured belly. But it was over. The stampeding animals had passed.

Jed dragged himself to his knees and then his feet, and walked over to the mule. Drawing the Peacemaker he put the animal out of its misery. The shot in their midst brought the encampment to order. The weeping subdued to a blubbering as mothers held children and husbands held wives. Every eye was on Jed Longman. He eased his shoulder, then stretched out a lump in his back.

'This won't be the end of it,' he warned. 'Keep those lamps shaded and let's see what can be fixed and who's hurt. Moynihan, take an inventory. Guards to your posts.'

Nobody moved.

'We ain't got time to gawp,' he called. 'Those animals were driven right up to our door. That means the bushwhackers who drove 'em are out there in the darkness just the other side of the wagons. Come on, stir yourselves. You want 'em in here with us?'

The men caught one another's eyes, uncoiled from their families, picked up rifles that had been dropped. It seemed to take an extraordinary long time. Jed peered round for Brookner, wondering if he had instigated this, but he couldn't see the man so instead he sought Mrs Harris and his boys.

'I didn't cry, Pa,' Jake said as soon as he neared them, though his large eyes stood testament to how close he'd been.

'You're a brave boy,' Jed said.

'They're all brave boys,' Mrs Harris corrected.

'Vern cried,' Jake said, 'but I didn't.'

'Crying is OK. It's only a fool of a man who ain't scared at a time like this.'

151

'You scared, Pa?'

'Sure am. Being scared is what keeps yer wits sharp.' He laid a hand on his eldest's shoulder. 'How you doing, Tom?'

'OK.' His voice sounded timorous. 'They coming back, Pa?'

'Don't know for certain. Probably, so we'd better be ready. Look out for your brothers now, and look out for Mrs Harris.' He stood to gaze at her so she wouldn't miss his meaning. 'She's a mighty fine lady, a brave lady.'

He hoped that she might say something, at least smile at him a little, but the moment was snatched from them by consternation at the barricades.

'Someone out there's calling. I can hear 'em!'

Jed was across there at a run. 'Dim those lamps! You want to get picked off?'

The lamps were pulled away and dimmed, throwing the men at the barricade into sharp relief against the wagon's side.

'Should we call back?' Moynihan whispered.

'No, keep quiet. Can anyone see any-thing?'

'Halloo there at the wagons! Can yer hear me?'

'Nobody answer,' Jed ordered. Men were crowding his shoulder. 'Keep the sentries watchful. This could be a trick to get in behind us.'

'Halloo there at the wagons! This is Baddell. How you folks doin'?'

Gasps erupted all around. 'Quiet!' Jed warned.

There was pushing to his right and he turned to snarl his irritation, only to find Mrs Harris forcing herself through the throng. He looked at her in astonishment. She looked back with a stony expression.

'Sorry about the mix-up,' Baddell was shouting. 'Didn't realize my kinsman was riding with yer...'

Jed felt his spine ooze perspiration.

'Kinsman?' Gunstead queried. 'Did he say *kinsman?*'

There was murmuring around him until

153

someone told them to hush.

''Course, that brother o'mine might not want to be owning up to the blood tie, 'specially as there's a price on his head same as there is on mine.'

The men crowding Jed were drifting back. He could feel space mushrooming all around him. Only Mrs Harris hadn't moved. Her eyes were as big as saucers and she was staring directly at him.

'Keeps a-calling hisself Marshal Longman so's no one–'

Jed never heard the rest in the ensuing hullabaloo, but he heard the click as a revolver's hammer was thumbed, and felt the muzzle press cold into his cheek.

NINE

Mrs Harris started to react, but Gunstead was waiting for her move and forced a rifle against her throat. The long shotgun she was carrying was wrenched from her grasp.

'What you doing to Mrs–' The revolver was rammed into the side of Jed's face. It felt as though his cheek had been punctured and it took all his stamina not to cry out. The weight of the Peacemaker was lifted from his hip and the weapon brandished beneath his nose.

'I knowed it – I knowed it all along,' seethed Brookner. 'What lawman has notches on his gun? Gettin' us to hobble our animals to set 'em up as targets. Ordering us to shoot our own critters as they was run into us.'

Each time he spoke he jabbed the tip of

the barrel into the side of Jed's face. Jed could feel the blood running down his jaw, taste it pooling on his tongue as the flesh inside his mouth was ripped over his teeth.

'You murdered the colonel. I knowed it. I *knowed* it.'

Moynihan stepped to Brookner's shoulder. 'Baddell's calling again, listen.'

Jed angled away from the prodding weapon. 'Moynihan, it's a trick. I ain't his–' The blow from Brookner's gun-barrel caught Jed across the eyebrow and sent him reeling against the wagon. He clung to the wheel as he clung to his senses. Baddell's syrupy tone floated into his consciousness.

'–so's we just like you to send him an' his out here so the family can all get acquainted again.'

'Like hell we will!' Brookner shouted back. 'We're gonna hang 'im, just like you hanged the Thompson boy. *Just* like that. You hears me?'

There was a noise, half-way between a scream and a caterwauling, and Tom rushed through the men wielding a wood-axe.

Brookner grabbed the shaft as Tom attempted to land the blow. Jed's eldest clung on, even when Brookner lifted him off his feet and swung him round to dash the boy against the wagon's side. Jed tried to intervene but was felled by a jab in the ribs from Gunstead's rifle butt. In the *mêlée* the wood-axe slithered across the ground to land at the feet of Mrs Harris.

'Don't even think about it!' Brookner snarled, his revolver levelled at her face. She said nothing, merely stared at him down the length of the barrel.

'Er, Mr Brookner, I feel–'

'Stop whimpering, Moynihan, an' pick up that axe, 'less you want her to put it through yer head. An' don't think she won't.'

Moynihan crouched down to retrieve the tool, holding it in front of him as if it was unclean. 'Don't you think, Mr Brookner, we might be–'

Brookner snatched it from his hands. 'Go find yer pen an' make yer inventories. You ain't the stomach fer a man's decisions. Knew it straight off, trotting behind the colonel like a hound.'

'Quiet back there!' hissed Dodd. 'I can't hear what's being called.'

Jed reached out to draw his son close in to him. There was a gash seeping blood somewhere above his boy's hair-line, and tears were silently streaming down his cheeks, but Jed didn't think that they were being shed because of his physical hurt.

'You did good, Tom, real good.'

Jed glanced above them. Gunstead still had Mrs Harris pinned to the side of the wagon by his rifle at her throat, but his attention was with everyone else's, beyond the barricade. Dodd was calling out to Baddell, saying that they couldn't hear what he was telling them.

'Listen to me, Tom. Shuffle behind Mrs Harris's skirt there, then roll under the wagon an' slip outside the circle. Get back to your brothers and take 'em out into the darkness, real quiet like. Follow the creek's flow to our wagon–'

'Pa...'

'I know, Tom, but listen good 'cos I'm relying on yer, yer brothers are relying on yer. Take from the wagon what food yer can carry an' hole up downstream. If I ain't there in two days keep walking. Got that?'

'Pa...'

Jed reached out to kiss his son's bloodied forehead, still damp from the fever, and patted him on the shoulder. The next moment he was patting air.

'–ain't right neighbourly,' Baddell was calling. 'We brung your cattle back to you so as you can leave all peaceable, an' I'd like my brother to return to the bosom o' his family. Fair exchange as I sees it. Besides, we got somethin' here you don't want...'

Moynihan stepped forward. 'Something we don't want?' Brookner waved him quiet.

'...Collected in fer a job, but we'll use it here if we have to...'

'What's he talking about?' Moynihan pressed. There was a rumble of concern

159

from the men around him.

'Dynamite!' called Baddell. 'An' yer got two minutes to send out my brother an' his kin afore the first stick lands in yer lap!'

Brookner moved like a man possessed, pushing aside the knot of men gasping and gaping at the news. He headed straight for Jed still sprawled on the ground.

'Where's the kid?' he demanded of Gunstead.

'Gone!' spat Jed. 'Yer ain't sending my boys out to that lying murderer to be butchered!'

Brookner roared his displeasure and aimed a kick at him, but Jed had hoped to goad the big man into doing just that and was ready to catch the swinging boot and yank him off his feet. Brookner's arms flew above his head as he went down and one of the two guns he was holding fired. Jed launched himself at Brookner's bull throat and got a grasp, but then he was seeing stars as Gunstead clubbed him with his rifle. Brookner was easily able to throw him off, and this time the aimed kick hit home, straight into Jed's kidneys.

'Get 'im tied, an' hobble 'im. I ain't having 'im running off. Her, too!'

Mrs Harris glared at Brookner but said nothing. To speak would give the man the excuse he wanted to hit her, and she needed her wits. Baddell was calling, accusing the shot of being fired out at him, and the men wanted Brookner to pacify him before a dynamite stick was lobbed into their midst.

As he made his way to the barricade Gunstead grabbed one of her hands and started to wind a length of rope about her wrist. She glanced down at Jed. He was groaning but his eyes were rolling in his head, and even though his limbs were seeking a purchase she doubted that he knew he was even trying. He certainly wasn't stopping Eli Thompson from binding his arms behind his back.

When Gunstead turned her about to grasp the other wrist she spun round to face him.

'Don't be an idiot!' she chastised. 'How am I going to keep him on his feet and hold a lamp to show we're coming through if my hands are tied behind me?' She offered her wrist and he took it. 'Give me some slack, too. I'll not be able to manage with my hands crossed, will I?'

Gunstead blinked, but did as he was bidden. Mrs Harris looked over his shoulder. Moynihan was watching, a grim look etched on his face.

'Are you not helping, Mr Moynihan? Not helping won't save you. When the Army's Board of Inquiry sifts through all the testimonies it'll be your name sitting at the top of the list as heading this company, poor Colonel Fremont having given his life to save others, God rest his soul.'

She saw his Adam's apple bob at the open neck of his shirt, but he didn't move and he didn't speak. Brookner was returning.

'Are they trussed? Throw a pail o'water over 'im and let's get going. Why ain't she tied proper?'

Mrs Harris caught hold of Gunstead's arm. 'Tell him,' she whispered.

'Er… She needs to hold a lamp. An' support him, too,' he said, his voice growing stronger as he spoke.

Brookner growled and tossed his hand in a dismissive gesture. 'Get 'er hobbled.'

There was a call from beyond the animals herded close for comfort. Mrs Harris felt her heart sink. The Longman boys were being dragged forward, Thomas's hands tied, Jacob being held by the collar but fighting all the way. Little Vernon was sobbing, his clothes dripping water as he stumbled behind his brothers.

'Found them skulking near the creek. Threw a stone at me when I hailed 'em.'

'Well, get 'em all tied in line an' let's be moving. Do I have to do everythin' myself?'

Water was thrown over Jed to bring him to his senses and he was pulled to his feet and dragged towards the barricade. The boys were lashed to Mrs Harris and a lamp pushed into her free hand. She looked across at Moynihan, biting his lip.

'Ever heard a person being tortured, Mr

163

Moynihan? Ever heard a child? It won't be Brookner's name heading that list, Mr Moynihan. Remember that. It'll be yours.'

Dodd reached forward and grasped her ties, dragging her towards the barricade. A hole had already been made in it for them to pass through. Jed was shaking his head, slowly coming round to consciousness. When he saw them approach his eyes grew large and he tried to throw off those holding him.

'No! Not my boys! You can't do this! He'll murder them. Don't you understand? Baddell will murder us all.'

Not a man spoke as Brookner tied his arm to that of Mrs Harris.

'He ain't gonna leave you be!' Jed shouted. 'When he's finished with us he'll burn you out!'

'Enough of that,' snarled Brookner and shoved him through the gap. Mrs Harris followed, pushing him from behind.

'Go, Jed, go! Stop fighting me!'

They stumbled out into a darkness lit only

by their lamp. Mrs Harris pulled harder, taking steps as big as her hobbles would allow.

'Thomas, take this lamp. Hold it out as far as you can reach so you won't get hit if one of them shoots at it. Jacob, lift my skirt. Quick, Jacob, I can't get to the knife.'

Jed stopped pulling back. 'Knife? You got a *knife* up your drawers?'

'Of course I have a knife. Why did you think I wasn't fighting back there? They would have found it in the tussle.'

'Sure,' mumbled Jed. 'I forgot. The great an' noble Mr Harris's *Art of Self-Reliance*.'

'Got it!' Mrs Harris started sawing at the rope linking her to Jed.

'Not me!' he snapped. 'Cut loose the boys.'

'Stop telling me what to do and start telling me your connection to Baddell. You never made a murmur back there when your being a marshal was denounced, but you soon spoke up when he called you his brother.' The rope linking her to Jed finally gave and with more movement now she sank down to start on her own hobbles. 'Well? There has to be a connection. All this doesn't stem from a drunken meeting in a saloon.'

'He's my uncle,' Tom said.

She looked at him in surprise, a thin figure holding the lamp, and then she turned back to Jed.

'Baddell is Martha's brother,' he explained, 'but there's no kin-love here. He's never forgiven me for taking her to wife and gettin' her killed 'cos some low-life couldn't get to me.'

The bindings at her feet snapped and she reached out for Jed's.

'Come on, Longman. What yer stallin' fer? You thinkin' o' doin' anythin' fancy, think again. Or do yer want a stick tossing yer way to help y' along?'

'He has no dynamite,' Jed said. 'He wouldn't have gone to the trouble of rounding up the animals if he'd had any.' He pulled away from her grasping hands. 'Not me! Save my boys.'

'I'm not leaving you, Jed.'

'You gotta. Between his bushwhackers and that bunch o'cowards back there we got nowhere to hide. If he's concentrating on me it'll give you time to get away. Tom, give me that lamp.'

'Pa, y' gotta–'

'Now Tom! Put the ring in my hand.'

'Longman…!'

Tom passed across the lamp while Mrs Harris cut into his bindings.

'There's no time fer that! Go! Do yer hear me, *go!*'

Her face angled towards his, the lamplight giving her features a harsh yellow tint.

'Go,' he whispered. 'For pity's sake, go.'

She didn't answer, but turned abruptly, her arm outstretched to gather in his boys. A glint from the blade was the last he saw of them.

'Longman … I ain't telling yer again.'

Jed lurched to one side, the lamp jiggling by his hip, hitting his empty holster. With his arms tied behind him it was the furthest he could hold it, but he was determined that it would be a beacon to lead Baddell away from his family.

'Yer drifting left, Longman. Yer ain't drifting left fer a reason, are yer?'

Jed slowed his pace. He hoped that Mrs Harris had covered enough ground. Baddell sounded closer. And then there was his gang to consider. Baddell was cunning. Perhaps he had second-guessed them and his men had been cast out like a net. There was nothing Jed could do about that now. His only hope was to distract them.

He moved forward slowly, breathing deep, trying to clear his mind. He pulled on the rope at his wrists wishing he had allowed Mrs Harris to cut into them more. He wished he'd let her cut his hobbles. He wished he had her knife.

There was a noise in the darkness, the whinnying of a horse. They were coming, drawn by the light.

He heard the animal's steady hoof-falls

and fought the urge to peer about him. Instead, he straightened his back and waited. If he was going to die, he was going to die with some dignity.

The circle of light was so small that Jed could smell the animal before its snuffling nose appeared. It kept on coming, step by tentative step, until it was close enough to lick him, until its rider entered the light.

His head was bowed, his hat pulled low, throwing his face into dark shadow. He stayed that way a moment, before lifting his chin. Jed saw the curving grin, the black eye-patch weeping lightning scars. He felt the steel grip of the man's one good eye.

'Hello, bro,' said Baddell. 'Miss me?'

Into the pool of light snaked a lariat. Jed saw it coming from his left and went down on his haunches, but the wide lasso en-compassed him. There was a cry to startle a horse. The rope bit and Jed's feet were taken from under him as he was dragged over the grass, Baddell's laughter echoing in his ears.

TEN

'How yer doin', bro?'

Jed opened his eyes a slit, but the lamp was held so close that he could see nothing beyond its yellow light. 'Ain't your brother,' he rasped, though the words didn't sound as he'd expected.

'What did he say?' asked a new voice. 'Perhaps I should rattle his teeth a little. Get his brains back into working order.'

'Yer don't touch him,' snarled Baddell. 'No one touches him. Understand? You all hear that? No one touches him but me.'

Jed tried to move his head to glimpse how many there were, and winced with new pain. Where Brookner had kept jabbing with the gun, his face was as swollen as a pig's bladder. The lamplight came close again, blinding his vision.

'My, my, what a mess yer are, bro. An' look at yer. What's this yer wearing?' Fingers plucked at the front of Jed's flannel shirt. 'I remember hand-stitched silk, an' a vest so fancy with gold roses that if a fella wasn't told he'd think yer were a gambling man instead of a lawman.'

'So he is a lawman,' gasped Scholl.

The lamplight receded. 'Dirt under my heel is what he is, what he always was, just too stupid to accept it.' The kick to Jed's boot was vicious and felt all the way up his leg into his groin.

'But if he's a lawman—'

Baddell laughed. 'A second-rate regulator for a second-rate freighting company was what he was, bought for the price of a bottle. Sheriff went an' broke his leg. Dep was a four-eyed ol'-timer deafer than a post, so they needed someone to walk the boards. That's what Longman here was, a board-walker in a fancy vest. Freightin' company was glad to off-load him. Profits sure increased. Surprised you didn't end up behind yer own bars, Longman. That would have a' been justice, don't yer think?'

So the rumours had reached even Baddell's ears. Jed struggled to a sitting position in an effort to ease his throbbing head. 'Never took a bribe.'

'What was that, Longman? Don't mumble down there in the dark like a prairie dog in its hole. Scholl, light another lamp an' let's not be missing any o' this. Tell it loud, Longman, so everyone can laugh. Never took a bribe, did yer say? Ha! Cheapest information ever bought. Boastful men are allus easy to tap. A sniff o' whiskey and his tongue wagged faster than one of McIntyre's Mex washerwomen.'

Squinting into the gloom, Jed tried to focus his blurred sight. Another lamp was being lit, another patch of ground illuminated. He could hear horses, restless and snorting. If he could just see them he might be able to tell how many Baddell counted in his gang.

'An' Longman had a vanity of such a size

that I could tell him anythin' come the mornin' hangover an' he'd lap it up like a calf to its mother's milk. Fill his pockets with silver an' tell him he'd cleared everyone round the table, an' he'd recall who he'd played and what cards he'd beat 'em with!'

Men chuckled. One giggled, a strange high-pitched sound that reminded Jed of the single time he'd met Golder in life, before his and Baddell's pictures started to adorn a law office wall. He'd giggled when Jed had offered his hand to shake, giggled and hid it behind a tight lip and dancing eyes. The recollection still caused a shiver down Jed's spine. The giggler in the dark wasn't someone he wanted near Mrs Harris, nor near his boys.

'Told him once he'd been breakin' a big mus-stallion the livery was keeping to service the mares. Told him how I'd *begged* him not to ride it, *begged* him with my life–' The men laughed louder at Baddell's theatrics. '–but as the Lord is my witness I said, he'd been such a dazzlin' horseman he'd stayed on its back as it had crashed through the rails setting the mounts free, finally tossing him against a fence-post and stomping him into the dirt–'

Jed remembered the story, though it hadn't been told to him quite like that. He drew his gaze from the man with the lamp and focused on Baddell, still acting out the part, kicking at the dirt with his toe, gouging it with his heel, as if a person lay there beneath his boot. No one was laughing now. Even the giggler was silent.

'–an' finally I swung him by the arm and crashed him into the fence-post, aiming to crack that pretty face o' his–' He broke off, breathing hard with his exertion. 'Mis-judged, didn't I? How is that shoulder o'yours, Longman? Still playing yer up, I hope.'

Jed couldn't separate that one pain from the others he was enduring, but he flexed the shoulder just to check if he could, flexed his fingers to be certain the blood pumped down that far, and he increased the tension on the bonds tying his wrists. Mrs Harris had started slicing at them, and he would ensure they frayed. He would need his hands free to tighten them round Baddell's throat.

'Got a decent price for the horses, too. Even spent a quarter to raise a glass to yer name. I'll wager yer didn't appreciate it. Not appreciating this, are yer? You will, though, you will. Just wait 'til the new Mrs Longman gets here. You'll appreciate it then. We'll all appreciate it then.'

Jed felt his mouth turn dry and his gut twist. He'd expected such a threat, but Baddell sounded so sure of himself.

'Come on, where's that lamp? We don't want her passing us by accident. An' get that fire going an' put on some coffee. It's gonna be a long night so we might as well enjoy a few comforts.'

'She won't come here,' offered an older voice, one Jed hadn't heard before, 'but the light might bring the wagon-folk down on us, right enough. We make as good targets as they did with a light behind us.'

Baddell sneered. 'The wagon-folk are cowering behind their stockade, an' they won't be coming out 'specially when the screaming starts. An' Mrs Longman an' the little 'uns? Where else they gonna go? Out on to the prairie to die o'hunger an' thirst? What you tell 'em, Longman? Hit the river an' follow it downstream?'

Scholl had trimmed the wick and replaced the glass, and the lamp burned bright now. He carried it away from Baddell, throwing his agitated form into stark silhouette.

'Never think further than the end o'your nose. That's allus been your problem, bro. Where d'ya think y'are? Texas?'

With awful certainty Jed knew where he'd been brought. As the lamp was carried through the night its light caught the edge of a pot, a pan, an upturned pail, until it was hung from a pole set through the spokes of a wagon's wheel – his wagon. He'd sent Mrs Harris and his boys straight into Baddell's arms.

Again Jed pulled against his restraints, but the ties wouldn't give. He needed to get his hands free; he needed a weapon. Desperately he began trailing his fingertips over the ground behind him, combing through the many stones for one with an edge. If he'd only let her cut him loose…

'Get on out there, Scholl, an' invite the lady in. An' watch yer manners. We don't want you partakin' afore yer turn.'

As the man skirted the wagon to drop down towards the creek, Baddell snatched up his lamp and came close, his sour breath pouring into Jed's face, his one good eye gleaming wide beside the patch covering the other.

'What's she like, Longman? Thin stick, is she, all bone an' spittle? Or is she as plump an' soft as a goose-down pillow? Baddell's finger poked him in the shoulder.

'Come on, bro, give us a taster of what's in store. Is she a moaner or does she just breathe hard? What does she like yer to do to her, eh, bro? Come on, I know you ain't shy. If you ain't gonna talk to me, there ain't no point in having a tongue in yer head. Might as well stick it in a skillet and sizzle it fer dinner. Gettin' tired o'yer mouldy bacon.'

Jed launched himself forward in an attempt to head butt Baddell, but the man was expecting it and stepped clear, leaving a trailing foot to snag Jed's hobbles and send him crashing to the ground.

'Ha! Like I says, never thinks beyond the end o' his nose. You're a sorry son of a whore, Longman.'

Spitting out grass and blood, Jed squirmed on to his back in an attempt to save himself from a follow-through kick, but his sleeve got snagged, and as he jerked it free the cloth tore. He was lying on something long and thin and made of metal, and the knowledge caused his heart to race. Baddell was advancing on him again. If he yanked him up Jed would never get the chance to grasp his weapon. He had to keep him talking.

'An' what does that make you?' he snarled.

'You know what happened to Martha, and you're setting to do the same to–' Jed snapped his teeth down on Mrs Harris's name, but Baddell was building a bluster of his own and didn't notice. It was a tool Jed was lying on. His fingers were catching on the rasping edge of a file.

'That were your doin', Longman. We were fine afore you came along to put yer feet under our table an' notions in her head. Didn't deliver on 'em, though, did yer? While you strutted the boards in your fancy vest she stayed in the same clay-floored shack breedin' squealin' piglets until someone comes gunning fer you and finds her instead!'

'Someone? Someone like who? Like these low-lifes y'got watching yer back here? You're as much to blame for what happened as me.'

Baddell seemed to shudder, his lips drawing back over his teeth as if he might bend down and rip a piece from Jed's throat. Jed hoped he'd try. He'd got the file in his fist now, its pointed end ready to wield as a blunt knife. Instead, Baddell's head shot up and he glared at his men.

'Why's that fire takin' so long?'

In one swift movement Baddell swung the lamp he held, throwing it towards the man squatting behind the first flickerings of flame. The glass shattered on the edge of the pit, its oil spilling and igniting with a *whoomph*, to light up the night. The man fell backwards, slapping at his legs with his hat and yelping like a dog. Jed rolled on to his side and brought himself up on to his knees, angling the file to razor it against his wrist-ties, using the sudden light to search out Baddell's men – three plus him and one down by the creek – and count the skittish horses tethered to the wagon. There were more horses than men. Where were the other men?

'When I say I want a fire, I want it *now!* Get some wood on there an' build up a good burn. Tear the wagon apart an' feed it to the flames; it ain't goin' nowhere. Sucklin' pig needs hot coals to do justice to its meat, an' we got some squealers comin' in.'

One of the men giggled. Jed marked him, marked his boyish features and his wide eyes. Another one like Golder. Jed hadn't been wrong. He tore at his bindings. One loop had snapped. Why couldn't he free his hands?

'There ain't gonna be no murdering children, an' no rapin' women.'

The words came slow and deliberate from the man sat back from the fire-pit. With more light to see Jed recognized him as one of those who had come to the wagons begging supplies and lying through his smile. He wasn't smiling now. Baddell swung round on him but it was a Mexican who voiced the warning tone.

'Señor Mac…'

Baddell lifted a hand and the Mexican was silenced. 'What was that, McIntyre?'

'The Devil sends his progeny to dwell among soulless men, and the Lord stands by and watches to test whether they're worth savin' or sendin' to the fires o'Hell.'

With difficulty he clambered to his feet, giving his still smoking pants one last brush with his hat.

Leaning back on his heels, Baddell took up a mocking stance, propping his fists on his hips. 'Is that right, ol'-timer?'

''Tis the Lord's word, right enough. Preached, but not adhered to by this lost soul. Well, it's gonna be adhered to now. We're done with standin' by an' watchin' the Devil's work. The boy you ripped apart, Wallace, the woman–'

Baddell's gun roared. Jed hadn't noticed him draw it, but he saw the flame spurt from his side and McIntyre spin on one leg before flopping like a child's rag-doll. Jed's bonds finally gave. He held his hands close into his spine, watching Baddell, his revolver poised. He might be free, but this was not the time to act. Instead he reached back to start sawing at his hobbles.

'Anyone else want to voice an opinion?' Baddell bawled out to his two remaining men.

The giggler moved from foot to foot, raising a hand to wipe at his mouth. His eyes were fixed on Baddell, but there was something strange in the way he held himself.

'You got ants in yer pants, Girvan?'

The giggler extended a finger from his lips and Baddell's levelled gun eased a mite. Jed followed the giggler's gaze out beyond Baddell's shoulder and caught the flicker of a pale skirt as it melted into the enfolding darkness. He looked back, praying that the men hadn't truly seen it. Baddell and Girvan stood either side of the dimming fire. The Mexican had disappeared into the night.

Jed's hobbles snapped. He didn't think twice. With a blood-curdling scream to warn Mrs Harris, he flung himself forward, the file held high in his fist. He saw Girvan's jaw drop, saw him pull his gun as Baddell began to turn. The air between them filled with smoke and a report so loud as to burst his eardrums. Jed wasn't sure if he was shot or not and he didn't care. He was deter-mined to reach Baddell and jab the blunt file into his throat, once, twice, as many times as it took. The bastard wasn't going to roast his boys, or defile Laura Harris.

ELEVEN

Air forced itself from his lungs before Jed felt the blow that winded him. He started to collapse over his buckling knees, then lurched as he was shouldered aside. The barrel of a revolver caught him across the knuckles, sending the file spinning from his grasp. He reached out, trying to catch it in mid-flight, not realizing that he was falling, too, until he hit the ground.

'Bro! I didn't know y'had it in yer, yer sonovabitch! Yer stabbed me, yer– Hey! What we got here, now?'

With the change in Baddell's tone, Jed fought for the strength to rise. A boot laid squarely between the shoulders pushed him back into the turf.

'Well, ain't you a dainty thing. So good to meet you at last, Mrs Longman. Come into the light here. We been waiting on yer.'

A swirl of pink and white trailed in front of Jed's eyes, and his stomach wrenched at the thought of what was to come. Then the realization spread through his fuzzy head that he'd never seen Mrs Harris wearing such a coloured skirt. Certainly she hadn't been wearing it when she'd escaped into the night with his boys.

Looking up he saw the Mexican holding the arm of a small woman, a close-brimmed bonnet hiding her face, her head bent into her chest. Jed knew immediately that it wasn't Laura Harris. The Mexican knew, too, for he was smirking as he grasped the crown of the bonnet to drag it backwards, lifting up the head and revealing a crop of dark hair.

'Tom!'

Ignoring his father, the boy defiantly wrenched free his arm and glowered at anyone who would hold his gaze. 'I've come to rescue my pa!'

The three men howled their laughter.

'And I've come to help him.'

The sound of a woman's voice brought them up short, the sight of the coach-gun pointing their way fixed their attention. Tom released the strings beneath his chin, and dropped to the ground, disappearing into the darkness before the Mexican discovered that he was holding only the limp bonnet.

'Goddamn,' intoned Baddell. 'That was a true move.'

'I'm so pleased you approve,' said Mrs Harris. 'I would hate to disappoint you.'

Baddell began the twitchings of a smile. 'Aw, ya ain't gonna disappoint me, Mrs Longman.'

'Oh my, and here I am disappointing you already. I'm not Mrs anything. I wasn't when we last met, and I certainly haven't been since. Let's say that I've been saving myself just for you.'

The sing-song lilt of her voice made the hairs lift on the back of Jed's neck. He wasn't the only one to think that something was amiss. Above him Girvan altered his stance. The easing pressure of the man's boot allowed Jed to shift his position on the ground. He couldn't spy the dropped file, but he gained a full view of the stand-off.

The Mexican beside him, Baddell was holding a neckerchief below his ear – Jed's spirits soared to see that he had caught him with the file – but he was holding the cloth with his arm across his throat, leaving his gun hand free. Fearful now, Jed looked to Mrs Harris. She was standing as school-ma'am straight as ever he had seen her, the coach-gun gripped with a cold determination he knew she possessed. An errant lock of hair had detached itself from its pins and was fluttering beside her cheek. These he knew and, despite himself, admired. What he didn't recognize, what he didn't like, was the way her eyes sparkled as she gazed at Baddell.

'Wondrous, isn't it, when fate takes a hand? I hide away with a group of wagon travellers because I hear it could be you shipping for a sutler further along the trail, and you fall into my lap like a disgraced angel from heaven. Perhaps the Reverend Harris was right. There is a God, after all.'

'Don't recall knowing a Reverend Harris,' Baddell mused. 'Don't recall knowing you, pretty as you are.'

'Me you know well enough, pretty as I am, so let me tell you about the Reverend Harris, as his part in this is almost as big as yours and may help to refresh your memory.

'The Reverend Harris made it his business to be useful to the army by taking charge of white captives rescued from the hostiles. For a fee, of course. He'd escort them back to their grateful kinfolk who would be persuaded to pay him a second handsome fee for their safe return. I made the mistake of telling him that I had no kin. That's when I discovered his side-line, what he referred to as "purging the savage from my soul".'

A smile eased up Baddell's cheeks. 'An' what did that entail, exactly?'

'Dragging me behind the wagon like a stock animal. Working me. Starving me.

189

Beating me with sticks and using me as his whore, then beating me again for tempting him.'

Jed couldn't believe what he was hearing. Why was she telling them this? Didn't she realize what they'd do?

Girvan giggled. 'Y'look well on it.'

'Better than the Reverend Harris,' she told him. 'Better than you.'

Jed saw the coach-gun swing in his direction and he clamped shut his eyes. The air filled with a deafening blast and the pressure on his back released as bloody rain splattered his head and arms and the ground around him. Only then did the giggling Girvan start to scream.

The Mexican was cowering behind an un-moved Baddell. Mrs Harris – Laura – had them covered and didn't look as if she had even blinked an eye. Jed rolled away from the flailing arms and kicking legs and glanced back at Girvan. His stomach was a mass of shredded cloth drenched in blood. His face, dotted as if he suffered smallpox, had ballooned in its contortions, with staring eyes and a gaping mouth issuing the most hideous sounds Jed had ever heard.

'It was you that shot Golder,' Baddell said in a flat tone.

'That was my pleasure,' Laura replied, 'though unfortunately he was somewhat closer and so, unlike your friend here, never knew what hit him.'

Baddell shook his head. 'Should have known it couldn't have been Longman's doin'. I take it Scholl won't be walking back into the circle with a few sticks o'wood and asking if the coffee's hot.'

'That's the acceptance of the Comanches. Male, female, white or black, live long enough to show an interest and they are more than willing to teach their … *arts of self-reliance.*'

'*Señora,* finish him so we can hear our thoughts, eh?'

'I think not. I find it soothing. It reminds me of the Reverend Harris when I tied the drunken sot to his own cooking-irons and lit a fire beneath him. And if I'd do that to him, think what I have planned for you.'

Baddell chuckled. 'Quiet, Castilio. You're safe where you are. Don't y'hear the lady? She got things *planned,* so she ain't gonna shoot and risk hitting me, is she?' His tone hardened. 'Especially as she's only left herself the one barrel.'

Jed drew breath in panic. 'Don't talk to him, Laura. Shoot him!'

'Laura, is it? Ah, it's the *future* Mrs Longman. Wasn't so far adrift after all, was I?' Baddell cocked his head and squinted at her. 'Don't remember a Laura, though.'

'Of course you do. You were younger then, mind. Had two good eyes that could twinkle with the power of the stars when you wanted to ingratiate yourself. *Miss Tranter* this … *Miss Tranter* that…'

Jed looked from one to the other. Laura was acting as if she hadn't heard him. So fixed on her revenge, she didn't realize that Baddell was fanning its flames ready to use against her. In the middle of talking Baddell would pull his gun and shoot, as Jed had seen him do already. Even if she managed to fire the coach-gun there was still the Mexican behind him. Jed needed a revolver to even the odds.

'Tranter Freighting!' Baddell exploded. He lifted the bloodied cloth from his neck and pointed at Girvan. Jed followed his line. The downed man would have a handgun, probably still in its holster.

'I put a bullet in yer pa's belly just like that an' had him watch as I wiped that prim little smile from yer face.'

'Leaving us both with a wagon full of goods as gifts for the Comanches while you and your *compadres* escaped with the best spoils.'

'Well, I wasn't leaving yer intact for those Comanch' to have all the fun, was I? How did yer find 'em after me? Yer did enough cryin' an' wailin' I'm surprised they didn't slit yer throat.'

Jed pulled himself closer to Girvan. His screams had eased to a moaning now, the agitated thrashing of his limbs no more than a weak stir. Like Golder before him the smell was enough to make Jed retch, but he reached across the bloody body to find the holster strapped at his hip. It was empty.

'How did you lose your eye, Baddell? Raping another woman, was it? A bullet would have taken off your head, and a sharp knife wouldn't leave such jagged scars down your cheek.'

Jed patted his hands into the thickening blood around Girvan's torso, desperate to find the fallen gun. The lamp hanging against his wagon's cover threw little light so far, and the uneven grass was full of hiding shadows. If Girvan had been pulling it free when the buckshot had hit him, his jerking arm could have arced it anywhere.

'Besides,' Laura continued, 'a man holds a blade flat to slice between another's ribs. It's a woman who holds a knife aloft to stab down with all her might. Especially if it's not a knife at all, but scissors.'

Jed lifted his hands and stared at them,

stared at the congealing, sticky blood coating his skin the way Martha's had when he'd held her lifeless body in his arms, with Jake and Vern whimpering in their cradles at her feet and little Tom at the door asking what was wrong. There'd been scissors on the floor, scissors so bloody with gore that he'd believed she'd been attacked with them. She hadn't. She had been defending herself.

Clenching his fists until the blood oozed between his fingers, Jed began shaking with the horror filling his mind. He raised his gaze as Baddell angled his head to peer at him. His lips drew back and he grinned, his one good eye shining with a triumph finally taken.

A roaring energy filled Jed's battered body. He was on his feet and over Girvan before Baddell had closed his mouth. On his first footfall time slowed to a turtle's crawl. He heard Laura's shout, but the sound was elongated like the returned echo of a call, and he couldn't tell what she said. Baddell moved on to his back foot as his hand went to his holster. It seemed to take a year or more for him to reach it, for the butt to fit into his palm, for his fingers to lift the weight, for his thumb to prise back the hammer. Smoke sailed in front of Jed's eyes. Hornets stung his leading arm. Cannonfire filled his hearing. His second foot hit the turf as Baddell knocked into the crouching Mexican. The muzzle of his drawn pistol wavered before belching fire into Jed's face.

The bullet tore across his cheek without a touch of pain and the world collapsed back into real time. Jed didn't care. His left hand locked around Baddell's gun-wrist as his right clamped about the grizzled throat, his broken nails tearing into the flesh as he forced back Baddell's head, wanting to rip it from his shoulders. Together they fell over Castilio. Baddell rammed in two jabs to Jed's ribs with his free hand before Jed rolled him, trapping his arm, and then saw Castilio's legs straighten as he clambered to his feet, the toes of his boots turning towards them.

In the deep shadow beneath the wagon, Tom squirmed towards a wheel, dragging behind him the long-barrelled pistol Mrs Harris had taken from the man she had knifed. Again Tom repeated her instructions in his head. He was to do nothing unless she had fired both barrels and the bushwhackers still lived. Well, both barrels had been fired and the bushwhackers weren't all dead, but what she'd asked of him no longer seemed as easy as pretending to be a girl. He wasn't sure that he could do it, and he felt a tear trace down his cheek. Cursing, he rubbed at his eye to clear it, then fed the long barrel through the spokes of the wheel to rest it on the hub, just as Mrs Harris had told him. He could see the Mexican crawling from under his pa and his uncle. He was standing up and drawing his gun. He was going to shoot his pa!

Tom fought with the hammer, using both thumbs to drag it back. He realigned the barrel between the wooden spokes, and recalled Mrs Harris's directions: aim for his middle, hold your breath and–

The heavy hand of a dead man fell across the barrel, dragging the gun from Tom's fingers. He was left staring into the face of a whiskered old man dribbling bloodied spittle.

'No, boy, y'might hit yer pa. Let ol' Mac take care o'it for yer, then he can go to Heaven, can't he, and have somethin' good to say when St Peter challenges him at the Gate.'

Tom swallowed hard as he watched the man heave up one knee and lay the barrel along its peak. He only seemed to have one useable arm. Tom knew that he'd been shot, he'd seen the bloody ring on the man's shirt just below his collar, but as he bent his head beneath the light of the lamp to gaze along the barrel, Tom's eyes widened to see his entire back glistening with blood.

'D'yer know the psalms, boy? The twenty-third? Say it real calm with me, now, so I gets a level bead, an' I'll rid the world o'that demon Baddell. The Lord is my shepherd...'

Tom began to mouth the words, his voice following on as he looked out to the very edge of the circle of light '...He leadeth me – *Mrs Harris!*'

Jed didn't see Castilio draw his gun, but heard the click of the hammer and he dropped his shoulder, dragging Baddell across him as a shield. Instead of a shot Jed heard a scream, Laura running in, wielding the empty coach-gun as a club. Baddell's manic face filled Jed's vision as his forehead came down, but he jerked his neck and the force of the head-butt grazed his wounded cheek.

Laura, Jed could only think of Laura. Castilio had a gun and Laura had too much ground to cover. Desperately Jed fought for a purchase among Baddell's clothing so he could lift him enough to force a foot beneath his body and hurl him into Castilio to ruin his aim. A misjudged knee only tipped

Baddell over on to his side and they rolled again. Jed's fingers found a knife in Baddell's belt and he grasped it ready to plunge it into his chest. But it wasn't a knife, only a half-sharpened stick. He raised it anyway, knowing that it would never break through the layers of clothing. Instead Jed brought it down in a wider arc, directly into the staring orb of Baddell's one good eye.

From deep in his gut Baddell's scream echoed up his throat to fill the night. His body convulsed, throwing Jed aside, his fingers letting the revolver fall as his hands flew to his face. Jed reached for the gun, grasped it, turned on his knees to level it at Castilio, but the Mexican was already falling, a neat hole in his forehead, his dead eyes wide open.

'...*He restoreth my soul...*'

A ragged volley of shots hit McIntyre, pinning him against the wagon's wheel, and a group of men armed with rifles tentatively walked into the small circle of light, Moynihan at their head. He gaped at the scene.

Laura advanced on him, her coach-gun club held ready.

'What are you doing here? Where's Brookner?'

Moynihan balked at the sight of her. 'There's-there's been a change. We heard … screaming.'

His gaze fell upon Girvan, still moaning, still moving. Moynihan walked over for a look, and put a bullet through Girvan's head. Baddell shrieked at the sound and scrambled to his feet, weaving blindly, blood trickling through his fingers as he damned the world and everyone in it. Moynihan raised his rifle again.

'Not him!' Jed shouted. 'Never him!'

While Moynihan looked on aghast, Jed staggered over to grasp Baddell by the collar and force him out of the lamplight into the night and a darkness of Hell that was all his own. Laura came to take Jed's arm, and together they listened until Baddell's cursing and raging faded to a murmur borne on the prairie wind.

The boys wrapped in quilts and asleep at his feet, Jed sat on a box discarded from his wagon. The Peacemaker Moynihan had given him lay across his thighs, the first light of dawn playing over the dead men's fingers etched so brutally into the rosewood handle. Laura looked at the scars and then at Jed.

'He marked us all,' she said. 'He marked everyone he touched.'

Jed nodded. 'Deep down I knew he'd had somethin' to do with it, but I never...' His voice faded. 'She was his *sister.*'

Laura didn't continue his train of thought. 'Moynihan isn't going on,' she told him. 'He's taking the wagons back, and you're going back with them. You're not fit enough to go on alone.'

Jed raised his head. 'I didn't know I'd be going on alone.'

Straightening her spine, she gave him one of her piercing school-ma'am glares. 'Mr Longman, your boys need a good mother, and their father needs a good wife, not someone who lies and murders and is wanted by the law.'

'The way I see it, where we're going there is no law, an' a bit of selected schooling in your *arts of self-reliance* wouldn't go amiss for growing boys. Besides, who'd there be to put my shoulder back in? To say nothing of getting this buckshot out of my arm.'

He uncurled his fingers, and after a moment's hesitation Laura placed her hand in his.

'Now don't go thinkin' I'm getting down on one knee,' he said. 'I'm hurting so much I can't even get off this box.'

The publishers hope that this book has given you enjoyable reading. Large Print Books are especially designed to be as easy to see and hold as possible. If you wish a complete list of our books please ask at your local library or write directly to:

Dales Large Print Books
Magna House, Long Preston,
Skipton, North Yorkshire.
BD23 4ND

This Large Print Book, for people
who cannot read normal print,
is published under the auspices of
THE ULVERSCROFT FOUNDATION